'I said, "It's all rush, rush, rush. We no sooner get somewhere than we're off again, we never have time to enjoy it."

"You know the deal," said Maggie.

I should have. She'd kept on telling me. Devon in ten days. But I couldn't see why I had to suffer because she chose to set such a killing pace.

"Come on Maggie, AUNTIE Maggie," I said. "It's my holiday, too. You're supposed to say, 'Niece, the world is your whelk'."

That got her attention.

"WHELK?"

"I don't expect you to run to oysters . . . "'

Clare and her Aunt Maggie make a most unlikely pair of travelling companions as they hurtle round the beauty spots of Devon. For Maggie is a journalist – on a working assignment with a tight deadline and an even tighter budget. Clare, on the other hand, is supposed to think of the trip as a 'holiday'. But she knows that it is really no such thing – she is just being kept out of the way while her mother is in hospital. And she has this odd feeling that something awful will have happened when she gets back home . . .

TRAVELLING HOPEFULLY

TRAVELLING HOPEFULLY

JUDY ALLEN

CORGI BOOKS

TRAVELLING HOPEFULLY

A CORGI BOOK 0 552 525146

First published in Great Britain by
Julia MacRae Books

PRINTING HISTORY
Julia MacRae edition published 1987
Corgi edition published 1989

This book is set in 11/12 pt Century Schoolbook by
Goodfellow & Egan Ltd., Cambridge

Corgi Books are published by Transworld Publishers Ltd.,
61–63 Uxbridge Road, Ealing, London W5 5SA, in Australia by
Transworld Publishers (Australia) Pty. Ltd., 15–23 Helles Avenue,
Moorebank, NSW 2170, and in New Zealand by Transworld
Publishers (NZ) Ltd., Cnr Moselle and Waipareira Avenues,
Henderson, Auckland.

Made and printed in Great Britain by
Cox & Wyman Ltd, Reading, Berks.

Contents

Chapter One

For some reason, the first bit about the trip I remember clearly is trying to get Maggie to carry my bag. It was the blue canvas shoulder bag, the one I use for school, and I'd stuffed it a bit too full. It wasn't only that it was heavy, it was that it had all sorts of lumps and pointed bits sticking out that dug into me. So I put it down on the path beside me and called out, 'It's your turn to carry this.'

We were in a ravine at the time, on a path with steps cut into it, beside a river. Maggie was further on down the path, crouching down to take a photograph.

She took no notice of me, and I couldn't tell if she'd heard or not. There was something peculiar about that ravine. It seemed to swallow up sound, and also light, so that everything seemed a bit unreal. And, of course, the water was making a noise, falling over big rocks and boulders.

I looked behind me. Three elderly tourists were leaning on the fence looking across the river at the mark on the rock that showed how high the flood had risen all those years ago. I could tell they were definitely not the kind to make off with someone else's bag. So I left it, and ran on down to Maggie just as she was putting the lens cap back on. She looked up at me, with her face all greenish in the weird light, and said, 'We're not taking turns. It's your bag.'

So she had heard.

I said, 'It's heavy.'

She said, 'You shouldn't have so much in it, then.'

She stood up. She's not all that much taller than me, but I was wearing trainers and she had on those red high-heeled sandals of hers, so she could look down at me.

I looked back at the bag. What with the walls of the ravine, and the trees growing out of them, it was really gloomy up there, but the bag was such a bright colour it glowed. It looked like a fat blue gas flame. I could feel the dent the strap had made in my shoulder. I said, 'I'm not picking it up again.'

She looked at me for a moment, then she said, 'It's your bag. If you want to chuck it away that's your decision. Nothing to do with me.'

And she turned round and began to walk away, towards the way out.

I waited, but she didn't stop. Her skirt swung as she walked – left right, left right.

'Listen, it's too much for me,' I called. 'I can't cope any more.'

I can still remember how my voice sounded, really small and sad. After all, I didn't even want to be on the trip in the first place.

But all Maggie said was, 'Heavens above, it's not as if you're being asked to find the source of the Amazon or something.' And she simply went on walking. Didn't even glance back.

As she reached the hut at the bottom, near the gate to the road, I remembered the terrible pictures we'd seen in the window on the way in. They were only scrubby old newspaper clippings but they showed what had happened to the town when the flood came. There'd been heavy rain and the water had collected up on the moors and then it had found the river, and joined it, and come down with it. It must have been forced through the narrow ravine like a stampede. It had hit the town like a bomb – smashed up houses, broken up the road, drowned people, and all at night, in the dark, when they'd least have expected it.

It must have been quite cold in the ravine because I can remember feeling the goose bumps coming up on my arms. It was more than thirty years since it had happened, but thirty years doesn't count as much to rocks and boulders, and I knew they remembered it. It was as if the memory was trapped in the ravine, like a ghost – a feeling of excitement and at the same time a feeling of watery stillness.

I didn't want to be left alone with it.

I chased Maggie and ran around in front of her so she had to stop, and I said, 'I'd be fine on a real expedition. One with some point to it.'

What I didn't like about Maggie then is that she wouldn't come out and fight. If she got a bit annoyed – and she must have been annoyed by then – she just put little pleats in the sides of her mouth and looked superior. 'Let's have this conversation in the car,' she said. 'We're running late.'

We'd only been away a day and a half at that

point and she must have said 'running late' a thousand times – well, fifty anyway.

'As for finding the source of the Amazon,' I said, 'you're hardly dressed for that. Mincing along in those silly red sandals.'

And then I got a real fright – and even Maggie jumped – because one of the rocks seemed to speak to me. 'That's not a very nice way to talk to your mother,' it said in a wheezy old voice, right in my ear. But of course when we turned round it wasn't really one of the rocks at all, it was one of the elderly tourists I'd seen at the top of the path. They'd all come padding down in their Hush Puppies without us hearing them, and this one had brought my bag with her. She handed it to me and I was so surprised all I could think of to say was, 'She's not my mother.'

Maggie quickly switched on one of her hundred watt smiles and started gushing – thanking her, and telling me to thank her, explaining that she's my aunt, and all that. It's odd, but I realize I didn't like Maggie at all then. Thinking about her then and thinking about her now is like thinking about two different people.

The woman smiled at me in an annoyingly forgiving way, and smiled at Maggie in an even more annoyingly sympathetic way, and the three of them went on, rocking a bit from side to side as they walked because they were quite fat.

Maggie didn't bother to keep her smile on when their backs were turned, and I knew I'd gone a bit far.

'It's OK,' I said, in my brightest and most positive voice, 'I will carry the bag.'

But Maggie just said, 'I know you will,' and

crossed the road to the car park without even
looking to see if I was behind her.

We couldn't get in to the car straightaway
because a Ford Capri had pulled right in and
blocked the passenger side, and though the Datsun parked on the other side had left enough
room, there were about a million people clam-
bering out of it and taking up all the space with
their open doors.,

There was a bit of a silence between us, so I
said, 'Where to now?'

'On to Lynton.'

I thought she was testing me. 'This *is* Lynton,'
I said.

'No, this is Lynmouth. Lynton's on top of the
cliff.'

I remembered, then, that there were these two
places, and I also remembered looking through
one of the guidebooks and seeing that there was
a cliff railway that went from one to the other.
While we waited for the Datsun to unload, I tried
to persuade Maggie we should go up in that.

I had plenty of time because the car seemed to
have been packed with an endless supply of
middle-aged women. No sooner was one of them
free than another pair of struggling legs would
appear, followed by a bowed head and shoulders,
and then the rest of the body. It was like watching several crumpled butterflies emerge from the
same chrysalis.

But it was no use, Maggie wasn't having any;
she said she knew the thing was there and that
was enough, she didn't need to ride in it. She said
we'd only have to come back down again for the
car and that would delay us. She'd got her vague

13

expression on and at first I thought she was still fed up with me, but later I decided it was just that she was thinking about something else. She often is.

I said, 'It's all rush, rush rush. We no sooner get somewhere than we're off again, we never have time to enjoy it.'

'You know the deal,' said Maggie.

I should have. She'd kept on telling me. Devon in ten days. But I couldn't see why I had to suffer because she chose to set such a killing pace.

'Come on Maggie, AUNTIE Maggie.' I said. 'It's my holiday too. You're supposed to say, "Niece, the world is your whelk".'

That got her attention.

'WHELK?'

'I don't expect you to run to oysters. See how reasonable I am.'

The people from the next car had got themselves clear, but were still stumbling about in front of it, counting heads or belongings or something.

As Maggie waited while I got in at the driver's side and slid across, she said, 'We'll get up to Lynton really fast and then have lunch somewhere nice, OK?'

And blow me if one of the women from the Datsun didn't hear her and say to her, all sympathetically, 'You do have to keep on the go to keep them amused, don't you?'

When we drove off I told Maggie I was going to set up evening classes in 'Minding Your Own Business'.

The road up to Lynton was horribly steep.

14

The engine made gasping noises as if it wanted us to know it was suffering.

'It's not wild about this gradient,' said Maggie.

'Is it going to pack up?'

'Don't even think it.'

So I thought about the ravine instead. 'You could have rebirth ceremonies there,' I said, 'like they do in parts of Africa. Suppose you'd been right in it, at the time of the flood, and you'd been swept out by all that water – don't you think that would be like being born?'

'No, I don't,' said Maggie, 'because you'd be dead. Drowned.'

'But if you'd survived, say?'

'You'll have to ask someone else. I've never had a baby.'

'You wouldn't know from having one, you'd know from being born yourself. I can't remember being born – can you?'

'Me?' said Maggie. 'I can hardly remember what happened yesterday.'

'There's a girl at school who says she can. She says one minute it was all red and warm and the next it was all bright and light and cold. Oh, and noisy. But she didn't mention the water.'

'I should think she imagined it,' said Maggie. 'I'm not convinced you can remember anything before you have the words for it.'

I said I'd ask the new baby as soon as it could talk. 'When do they talk?'

'It varies. I think girls talk sooner than boys.'

'We don't know what this one is,' I said, as we crawled and wheezed up the road. 'Normally they can tell when they do the scan, but it had its legs crossed so they couldn't see. I think that's

15

nice. I don't think we should spy on it until it's ready.'

'What do you want? Brother or sister?'

'I don't mind. One of each'd be nice, but no chance. They say it's definitely a solo act, not a duo.'

We finally made it up to the top and when Maggie had settled the car into yet another car park she suggested I stay in it while she looked round quickly. It did seem like a good idea. She was the one who had to write the article, not me. She said that afterwards we'd go on to Martinhoe to look at a motorcycle museum. I thought she was pulling my leg, but she said she wasn't. She put the aerial up for me as she passed, so I could listen to the radio, and I stuck my head out of the window and said, 'Suppose as you walk round you bump into an enormous creature with eleven legs and seventeen eyes and green leathery skin and pointy ears?'

'I very much doubt if I will,' said Maggie.

'But if you did – you'd always remember it, wouldn't you?'

'I think I can safely say that I would. Why?'

'Just proving to you,' I said, 'that you can remember things before you have the words for them.'

Maggie actually grinned. Then she said, 'That doesn't prove anything. I may not have the word for the creature, but I have the words for "eleven legs" and "seventeen eyes" and all the rest . . . '

She began to walk away.

I got free of my seat belt and reared right out of the open window and shouted after her, 'I bet you remembered Grandma's face before you had the words for it.'

Maggie stopped, just for a moment, and then, without looking back, she raised both her hands and made a pair of clear thumbs-up signs above her head.

She wasn't gone long and when she came back she was all distracted again, and a bit out of breath. 'Apparently I should take a look at the Valley of the Rocks,' she said, 'just along the coast from here.'

'Who says?'

'Some woman who saw me taking pictures and asked what I was up to.' She hung over the back of her seat and picked out the map from the cardboard box full of guidebooks.

I found the place first. It was on the way to Martinhoe. 'Right,' said Maggie, pushing the map at me and starting the engine.

'I thought we were going to have lunch,' I said, with some difficulty because my head snapped back as the car shot out of its parking space.

'They don't close yet,' said Maggie. 'We'll just have a quick look and then double back. There's a place just off the A39 we can eat.'

I said why didn't we keep on to Martinhoe and eat lunch there and she said we weren't going to Martinhoe.

'You said we were going to see a motorcycle museum there.'

'That's at Combe Martin.'

'*You* said Martinhoe.'

'Did I?' said Maggie. 'Sorry. I get the names muddled.'

Getting dragged around at high speed by someone else is bad enough, but when you find out they don't even know what they're doing . . .

I said, 'You know this county like the back of your neck, don't you? Are you sure you're the right person for this job?'

Maggie ignored me.

I think the Valley of the Rocks might be quite nice if you were allowed to look at it for long enough to get your eyes in focus. They're like a group of small mountains that grow out of the turf at the top of the cliffs. The turf's green and springy, but scattered with stones – a great place for cartwheels if you had thick gloves on. I liked being on top of the world instead of deep in a ravine, and the air smelt so clean and good I kept forgetting to breathe out because breathing in was so nice. There were gulls gliding above the sea, and some of them were drifting up above the edge of the cliff and over my head. The sun seemed to shine right through them, between the long feathers of their spread wings, so that they looked transparent; fresh from the glass animal maker.

Maggie was messing about with her notebook and camera and I was looking up at the highest rock when I noticed a hairy little face looking back down at me from a crag. 'Hey!' I said, 'there's a goat up there.'

'Oh sure,' said Maggie, without looking up. 'Wolves, too, probably.'

'There is a *goat* up there,' I said. 'A little silky mountain goat.'

Well, of course, by the time she'd got the telephoto lens on the camera, the goat had got bored and gone round the other side of the rock, and at first it didn't look as though I was going to be able to persuade Maggie to walk round and

18

find it. But then I dug out one of the guidebooks and read out the description of the herd of wild goats. So when another couple of them came trotting round the rock on a little goat-path, and looked down at us to see if we were going to appreciate them better than we'd appreciated their friend, Maggie consented to look in the right direction, and even took a picture or two.

After all, if they were written up in a guidebook, even Maggie had to admit they must be there.

But just as I was thinking this was a likely spot for a picnic, we were in the car and off again, and next thing we were at some thatched farmhouse which had been converted into a pub. The restaurant was full, so Maggie went to the bar for something and I kept places at a rustic table beside a duck pond. She came back with two plates of ham salad, a glass of Coke and a glass of red wine. She sat sideways on to the table and ate her salad with one hand while she wrote in a notebook on her knee with the other.

'Pig salad,' I said, looking at the bright pink slices. 'I like pigs.'

'Good,' said Maggie, not looking up, writing.

'I mean I like them trotting about, not sliced.'

Maggie did look up then, 'Does your voice *ever* stop?' she said, but not nastily.

I told her that's what my dad says sometimes. I picked up a bit of meat on my fork. 'Sorry, pig,' I said.

'Do you think,' said Maggie, returning to her notebook, 'you could possibly just eat it and not try to form a relationship with it?'

'If I can,' I said. 'Where are we staying tonight?'

Innocent question, you'd think.

19

'I don't know,' said Maggie.

'Seriously,' I said.

'Seriously, I don't know,' she said.

Things were obviously worse than I'd thought.

I said, 'You mean we're not booked in any-where?'

'We'll find somewhere.' She wasn't concentrating at all, or at least only on what she was writing.

'We were booked in last night,' I said.

'You can on the first night out,' said Maggie. She sipped some wine, but she still didn't take her eyes off the notebook. 'But by the second night you can't tell where you'll be.' She crossed something out and wrote something else in.

I could see I'd have to get her attention before I'd get any sense out of her. I said, 'Did you know that drinking red wine makes your teeth go black?'

That did it. She looked a bit startled and lost interest in her notebook and started scrabbling in her bag for her mirror.

'It hasn't done it yet,' I said. 'It builds up. Suppose we can't get in anywhere?'

She clenched her teeth at herself in the mirror and then tucked it back into her bag. She still looked a bit distracted. 'We'll get in,' she said. 'The weather's dodgy, it's cheaper to go abroad, it's a bad season. Everywhere's half empty.'

'How can you say that when the restaurant here's full?'

'Restaurants are different. They get fuller in dodgy weather. Haven't you ever travelled on spec before?'

'Dad always books.'

'He would,' said Maggie. 'They've never got on.

'I know you don't want me here,' I said. I surprised myself . . . I hadn't really meant to say it – or anyway, not just like that.

'Don't be silly.'

'No I'm not being silly. I overheard Dad talk you into it. I didn't mean to. I was up in my room, but he was talking quite loudly.'

Maggie made an important business of putting the notebook away in her bag, just so, even turning it round so it faced a particular way. 'To be honest, I wouldn't have thought of inviting you,' she said. 'But I'm very happy to have you along.'

'Thank you,' I said, because I didn't really mean to be nasty to her. 'But I know you'd rather I was at home, and so would I. I really don't like this rushing around, not knowing where we're staying or what we're at or anything.'

'I can't change that,' said Maggie. 'I have to earn a living.'

'You could put me on a train home, though,' I said.

Maggie didn't answer at once. I couldn't decide if she was offended or considering the possibility. 'It isn't just that I'm not suited to this sort of trip,' I said. 'It's that it's so peculiar, this sending me away. They've never done it before. I feel as if something's going to happen while I'm not there.'

'Well – the baby . . . ' said Maggie.

'That's not for three weeks.'

'Well – but your mother's got to stay in hospital from now until – after . . . '

'I know, but Dad and I managed when she went in to have that cyst removed, and I was younger then.'

21

Maggie seemed very edgy. She'd given up on her salad and finished her wine and I guessed the problem was that she wanted us to be on our way. 'Things are difficult for your father at work . . . ' she said.

'They've been difficult for two months, it can't be that.'

I suddenly really wanted to tell Maggie, or someone, exactly what I was worried about, but I was afraid it sounded stupid so I fiddled around with the Coke glass while I said it, and didn't look at her.

'I have a sort of odd feeling,' I said, 'that when I get back I'll find something awful's happened.'

Then I looked up and I thought I saw a funny expression on Maggie's face, but it passed so quickly I couldn't be sure. 'That *is* odd . . . ' she said, but at that exact moment a man clonked a tray of beer and sandwiches down on to our rustic table, which was for four, and said, 'Is this seat free?'

One of the things I hate about travelling around is the way people creep up on you.

He was quite young, and not bad looking in a fat sort of way. He had on a suit so he must have been travelling on business, he can't have been on holiday. Maggie began to collect up her things. 'Yes, quite free,' she said. 'We're just off.'

'Oh,' he said, sitting down. 'I don't want to disturb two such lovely ladies.'

That cheered me up because I thought he must think I was a grown-up too, but Maggie didn't seem impressed.

'You're not disturbing us,' she said, quite calmly, but not smiling. 'We were just on our way.'

'No, no,' said the man, smiling a lot. 'You must let me buy you both a drink to show there are no hard feelings.'

'Why should there be any hard feelings?' said Maggie, standing up.

'I insist,' said the man, and he stood up, too, and he picked up Maggie's empty glass. 'Now this was red wine,' he said, twirling the glass by its stem under his nose, 'and what was your sister drinking?'

If he didn't recognize three inches of Coke in the bottom of a glass, I thought, he couldn't be as sophisticated as he pretended.

'No thank you,' said Maggie. 'Don't forget your bag, Clare.'

I already had hold of it, so I realized she wasn't really saying that, what she was really saying was, 'Come on, let's go.'

'Oh, now don't walk out on me,' said the man, putting on a joke-sad expression. 'I so rarely find such charming company.'

He was still standing there, still holding the empty wine glass. Maggie began to walk past him on one side and so I began to walk past on the other. He put his hand on her arm, quite lightly I think, but she looked down at it as though he'd stuck an old bit of chewing gum on her, so he took it off again, quickly. 'Do something rash, just for once,' he said, smiling, smiling, smiling. 'Join me for half an hour. You and your lovely chaperone. Otherwise I shall be forced to drink alone.'

'I'm sure you've had plenty of practice,' said Maggie, and she smiled, too, but it wasn't one of her hundred watt jobs, more like forty watts and the bulb about to go.

23

He stepped back to show us he wasn't going to stop us. His smile went off and then came back on again. He seemed to be taking it quite well, I thought. He even gave her a wink, and then called out as we walked away, 'You know, I like you.'

And Maggie said, over her shoulder. 'How nice. What a shame it isn't mutual.'

When we were back in the car I felt I had to say something. 'It's no wonder you haven't got a man,' I said. 'You just don't treat them right.'

But Maggie just laughed at me. 'Never mind classes for "Minding Your Own Business",' she said, 'I'm going to give you classes in "Creep Spotting". Much more useful.'

Chapter Two

Maggie did find us somewhere to stay that night.
There was a book with bed and breakfast places
in it among all the guide books and maps in the
cardboard box on the back seat, and she found us
a big, old, thatched farmhouse, down at the end
of a stony track, in a dip, among fields. There
were three cows in the nearest field, sheep up on
a kind of ridge, hens in the yard, a few sheds and
barns standing around, and an apple-cheeked
farmer's wife.

After a day of driving around Devon lanes, I
was feeling a bit apple-cheeked myself, but mine
were green Granny Smith's and hers were red
Worcester Pearmains.

I was really impressed at first. I thought Maggie had finally found the true Devon, and she
could write whatever she was supposed to write
about it, and we could both relax and go home.
But when I suggested that, she just said she
wasn't expected to write about accommodation,
and when we really got into things, it wasn't
what it seemed, anyway. The only field that went
with the farmhouse was the one beside the track,
with the heifers in it, the rest belonged to the
farm out of sight beyond the ridge. The barns
were rented to a different farm, in the other

direction, and the genuine Devon farmer's wife came from Leicester and was married to a travelling salesman. Also, from close to you could see the apples in her cheeks came out of a jar marked 'Blusher'. The hens were hers, though. She'd been a professional bed and breakfast landlady for three years, she said, and this was the worst season ever, and yes we could have separate rooms, two each if we liked.

Perhaps she and her husband spent all their money on winter holidays, or perhaps they just didn't have any, but they certainly didn't spend a lot on the house. The bedrooms were huge and they hardly had any furniture in them – just a double bed in each, one of those wardrobes with hangers on one side and shelves down the other, and a wooden chair. There was a dangling light cord over each bedhead, which worked the centre light, but no bedside light or bedside table.

I could tell Maggie wasn't knocked out by it because she whispered to me, 'All very clean, isn't it?' which is what Mum says about a place when she can't find anything else good. 'Well there isn't much to get dirty,' I whispered back.

But the non-farmer's wife, Mrs Vosper, obviously assumed we'd stay, so we did. She asked if we were on holiday and I listened with interest to hear Maggie's answer. I don't think I really understood at that point what she was doing, and it had got too late for me to ask her myself. I was supposed to know. But all she said was, 'Yes. Touring around. Taking a bit of a break.' So that didn't help me much.

I chose a room that looked out over the field with the little heifers in it – and I don't think I realized how damp it was until it was time to go to bed. There was a distinctly musty smell in the air, and when I looked closely at the wallpaper I could see that in most places it was bulging away from the walls. If even the wallpaper didn't want to touch the walls, it didn't look good.

Maggie may be Mum's sister, but they're not a bit alike. I knew Mum would never let me sleep in a damp room. I wasn't sure what damp was supposed to do to you, but I think I thought it grew moss on the insides of your lungs.

Anyway, then I thought maybe the bed was damp, too, because I knew that was supposed to be the real killer. That probably grew moss on your bones as well as your lungs. I turned back the covers to see if perhaps Mrs Vosper had put in a hot water bottle. And there, sitting in the middle of the bed, just below the pillow, was not a hot water bottle, but the biggest spider I'd ever seen. It was just sitting there, with its legs sticking up and then back down again, the way they do, as if it had its knees bent and arms akimbo all at once.

It gave me such a fright I shouted, 'Get out!' at it, but it didn't even twitch. They may be deaf. Perhaps with all those legs and all those eyes there's no space left for ears.

It looked awful against the white sheet.

I stood as far away from the bed as I could and stretched out one arm and tweaked the pillow. The spider ran, as if to go down under the blankets. So I grabbed the sheet and all the bedding and pulled the whole lot back onto the floor. It was very heavy, Mrs Vosper didn't run to duvets. The spider stopped and crouched again, as if it was menacing me, except that I think it had its back to me. How can it be necessary to have so many legs? Four would be quite enough.

I looked around for something to use to push it off the bed, but the only thing light enough to pick up was the chair, and that seemed a bit extreme. Chairs are for lions, not spiders. And I certainly wasn't going to use anything out of my luggage.

I did think of going to fetch Maggie, but I decided that was a bit weedy, so I picked up the pillow and banged the bed near the spider with it, and it ran to the edge away from me and then lost its footing (footing, footing, footing) and fell on the floor.

For a minute I couldn't see it, then I caught sight of it, legging it towards the door. I leapt around the bed with some idea of opening the door and chasing it out into the corridor, but it changed direction and made for the wardrobe. That wardrobe didn't stand more than a quarter of an inch off the floor, but the spider ran for the gap and then flattened itself out like the spokes of a wheel and worked its way underneath and out of sight.

I dug around in my case and found a pair of socks and laid them flat in front of the wardrobe and then worked them into the gap until they filled it up. Then I found another pair and worked them in under the end of the wardrobe at the side. The other side and the back were against the walls.

'I'll let you out in the morning,' I said to it. 'Go to sleep.'

I know they're supposed to be as frightened of

28

us as we are of them, and I didn't like to think of it under there with all those knees knocking but I couldn't think what else to do.

I put the bed back together again and got into it, but I didn't feel very sleepy.

Maggie had given me a copy of the magazine she's working for, so I had a look at that. It was called *Holiday UK* and the copy she'd given me had 'London' printed across one corner and a colour picture of the Horse Guards riding through Hyde Park on the front. There was a great long article by Maggie inside, that went on for about six pages, with lots of photographs, each with her name up the side of it. Then there were a couple of pages listing places to eat, theatres, cinemas, that sort of stuff. But most of it was adverts for hotels and restaurants and shops. Also it was free, so I realized it couldn't be up to much.

Still, I knew they must somehow have enough money to pay Maggie, or they couldn't make her rush around the countryside like a maniac.

The speed thing certainly wasn't getting better. The only time I'd managed to have a good look at something I wanted to see had been at a place called Watermouth Castle.

Maggie had been all for buying a brochure, having a quick look at the outside, and then aiming the car at the next place on. But I liked the look of it, so I ran ahead, bought myself a ticket with my own money, and went inside. Maggie couldn't very well go off without me, so she had to buy herself a ticket and follow me in. She made sure I kept on the move, but even so I did see everything. The best bit was down in the

29

dungeons where they had life-sized models of famous characters – like The Hunchback of Notre Dame – which began to move as you came near, almost as though they knew you were there. At the end you had to go through a Smuggler's Lair, and I won't tell you what happened because I expect you'll see it sometime and I don't want to spoil it, but even Maggie screamed. Then she said she thought the whole place could seriously damage your mental health.

The trouble with Maggie is – she doesn't know how to have any fun.

The rest was just a blur of twisty lanes and seaside cliffs and Maggie leaping out of the car and rushing into a restaurant to talk to someone for three minutes and then rushing back again with a menu. I could tell she felt she'd got back to normal life.

We were hurtling in one direction, which made the scenery seem to be hurtling in the other direction, and the only thing that stood still was an island out on the horizon. I found it reassuring, the way it just stayed there, and grew slowly as we worked our way along the coast. Maggie said it was Lundy, which means Puffin Island, and that it was a bird sanctuary. I didn't ask, then, if we could go there, because somehow it didn't look as if you could. It looked the kind of place for people with their own boats. So I didn't feel cheated out of Lundy, but as for the motorcycle museum – well we did go to it, but the bikes might just as well have been going full throttle round Brand's Hatch for all the detail I saw in our quick jog in at one side and out at the other.

I asked Maggie if she didn't ever get tired of doing everything so fast, and she said she did. So I said could we go a bit slower, and she said not really, because we had to do all this and get to Ilfracombe tomorrow morning. I said I supposed we only got a day in Ilfracombe and she looked amazed and said we'd need to leave by coffee time. When Maggie says 'coffee time' she means eleven o'clock, she doesn't mean you actually get to have coffee or a squash or anything.

When I chucked her *Holiday* magazine on the floor and pulled the cord over my bedhead it went dark, totally dark. That's one of the things I hate about the country, no street lights. It's much easier to worry about things in the dark, because there's nothing to take your mind off them. Still, that night I felt comforted because I thought Dad knew where we were and had our telephone number. In the morning I felt differently about it, but that night I felt comforted.

Maggie had tried to ring him in the evening, but he had been out – at the hospital, we'd guessed. So she'd rung the hospital and the sister had said he'd just left to go home. It was a busy time on the ward and there was no one free to take a portable phone to Mum, she said, but Mum was fine – and then she took down the number in case Dad needed to ring us about anything.

Maggie didn't call from the farm, she rang from the place where we had dinner. Mrs Vosper didn't do dinners. She did a farmhouse tea at six o'clock, she said, if it was wanted. It was nice to think she didn't do it if it wasn't wanted. But we'd missed that, and anyway Maggie is very conventional about meal-times – can't feel hungry before eight at night, by which time I'm almost chewing the furniture and everything's beginning to remind me of food. Even the car dashboard looks like a chocolate vending machine to me at times like that.

We went to a pub. Thatched, of course, I'm not sure Devon has any other kind. It had a separate restaurant, so I was allowed in. I think the idea is that children are not corrupted by seeing people drinking too much as long as we can see them eating too much as well. I had fish, and they took the head off for me, because I don't like the way they look at you. Maggie had steak. She ordered a bottle of red wine, but she only drank about half a glass and when we left she took the rest with us. They didn't seem to mind.

So while I was fending off the spider and tossing and turning in my damp bed, Maggie was in her room drinking wine and writing up the day on her battery-operated electronic typewriter, which is about the size of a thick tablemat and doesn't make any noise at all. It was very obvious that one of us was having a much better time on this trip than the other, I thought, but I didn't know what I could do about it.

Thinking about it made me feel tired and, although I didn't expect to, I went to sleep – thinking that at least Mum was OK. And Dad. It wasn't till the morning that I realized neither of us had actually spoken to either of them.

Chapter Three

The farm may have been a bit grim to go to
sleep in, but it was lovely to wake up in. There
had been rain in the night, but it was over by
the time the sun came up, and everything
sparkled. As soon as I was dressed I went
outside. The birds were singing. The little cows
were being led in from their field by a very old
man who looked like Father Christmas in a flat
cap. The hens were doing robotic dancing in the
yard.

I said hello to the old man with the cows, but
he didn't answer me. Later Mrs Vosper said
that he had worked here since it was a proper
farm, and he hadn't liked the fields being sold
off, and even more he didn't like there being
summer visitors. So he usually pretended they
weren't there.

Maggie joined me in the garden. 'You are
packed?' she said.

An awful thought struck me. 'We're not leaving before breakfast?' I said.

Maggie looked at me for a moment, and then
she grinned. 'No, no, of course not,' she said. 'I'll
go in and see how soon we can have it. In the
meantime, you can be bringing your bags down
and leaving them by the car.'

She *had* been going to rush off before breakfast, I could tell, but it seemed even Maggie couldn't carry cruelty to children too far.

I went upstairs and put back the few things I'd taken out of my big bag and zipped it up. I considered rearranging the blue bag, so it wouldn't be so heavy and lumpy to carry, but there was nowhere else to put the stuff, so I gave up. I put the bags outside the room and then, last thing, I worked the socks away from the edge of the wardrobe with the toe of my shoe. Nothing ran out. I looked at the socks lying in a crumpled heap on the floor and they gave me a funny feeling. I couldn't help thinking it might have got itself inside one of them and gone to sleep. I'll leave the socks there for the moment, I thought, and come back for them after breakfast. I knew I wasn't going to come back for them, but it helps to lie to yourself sometimes.

For breakfast we had scrambled eggs from the hens in the yard, tomatoes home-grown in the lean-to greenhouse at the back, and mushrooms that Mrs Vosper *said* she grew in the cellar, in buckets of special mould, but I wouldn't be at all surprised if she'd found them on the bedroom walls. They were nice, though.

It was all so different there, and the food was so good, that I forgot I was worried about home until we were on our way. Then what began to nag at me was the way the hospital had taken our number. What was the point of that if Dad had already gone home, unless they thought he might be called back suddenly or something? And was it really possible that they were too busy in the ward just to take a telephone to Mum?

'Can we ring the hospital?' I said, as we drove away from the farm. I'd noticed the day before that there seemed to be plenty of public telephone boxes standing around in hedges.

'It's better to ring during visiting hours,' said Maggie. 'We'll try this afternoon, if you like.'

'Well – can we ring Dad?'

'He'll have left for work by now. He's going in very early at the moment.'

'*At* work then?'

'Not a good idea,' said Maggie. 'If his job is to survive the take-over, the last thing he needs is a personal call. Doesn't look professional.'

'Not take-over.' I reminded her. 'We're not supposed to call it that. It's a merger.'

'Help! Police! Merger! Merger!' said Maggie

She was in an annoyingly good mood and didn't seem to me to be taking it seriously at all.

'Do you think he will lose his job?' I said.

'Well,' said Maggie, 'when a large company takes over a smaller one – sorry, merges with it – there are inevitably more people than jobs. Some'll have to go.'

'You sound very cheerful about it.'

'Sorry,' said Maggie. 'I think it's the effect of eating breakfast. I don't usually bother. It's surprising how much energy it gives you, isn't it? Also, I think summer's really started. Look at that sky. Pure blue. All that skim of cloud has gone.'

'He's working very hard to keep his job,' I said stiffly. 'Mum and I have hardly seen him for weeks.' I really did want her to know how hard he was working, but also it was much easier to worry about him and his job than about Mum

35

resting in hospital, gathering her strength to have the baby, and not even able to get to the telephone.

'Oh, he's hanging on in there.' said Maggie. 'Let's not worry about him on such a nice day. He's doing what he can, and there's nothing we can do to help.'

I wouldn't have minded her being like that about it, I don't suppose, if it wasn't for knowing that she doesn't really think much of him. It's easy not to worry about people you don't get on with. It seemed to me very important to let her know that he doesn't think much of her, either.

'Dad says you've never really made it,' I said.

There was a bit of a pause. We'd left the side roads and got on to a main road and I suppose she needed to concentrate. Then she said, 'Never made what?'

'Well, you know, *made* it.'

'Never made a Fair Isle jumper?' said Maggie. 'Never made a model of the Golden Gate Bridge out of Lego? Never made a black pudding?'

There he was, in the office all hours, getting tired and cross, and she was driving all over Devon doing what she liked and as cheery as anything.

'You know what I mean,' I said. 'Never really got there.'

'Never got where?' said Maggie.

'Well – anywhere.'

'I've got here,' she said, waving at a sign we were passing that said *Welcome to Ilfracombe*. 'That'll do for now. And don't try to manoeuvre me into a row with someone who's several hundred miles away.'

36

As it turned out we were more likely to have a row about Ilfracombe than about anything else. It's a terrific place. It's got everything. It's got cliffs, not too high, that stick out into the sea, and a harbour with boats and all that. And there's a long sea front with all sorts of places to eat and places to get ices, and a swimming pool and an ice-skating rink and shops with beachballs and buckets and things hanging outside, all up and down the door frames. It wasn't that I wanted to buy anything like that – perhaps Maggie was afraid I did – it was just that they looked so pretty and sort of happy . . . And the sun was shining and there were lots of people about, and they were all wearing colours as bright as the beach balls. We had a quick sweep around in the car before we parked, and there was a great feeling of things going on, things to do.

I couldn't wait to get out, when we did park, but as I did I glanced at Maggie and she had pleats in the sides of her mouth again, and she said, 'I knew it would be like this.' It was obvious she didn't think 'like this' was a good way for it to be.

'What's wrong with it?' I said, amazed.

'Full of trippers,' she said. And she looked amazed, too, as if the problem should have been obvious.

'But we're trippers,' I said.

'You may be,' said Maggie, grudging her camera out of its case. 'I'm at work.'

Then she tried to make me understand what a holiday place should really be like – and I tried to make her understand what a holiday place should really be like – and neither of us got anywhere.

Maggie likes everything oldy worldy, tiny coves

and dingly dells and thatched pubs and cute tea rooms – and, ideally, no one else around at all. Me, I quite like other people around. Apart from anything else, the more people there are, the more things there are to do. I like eating places that aren't pubs – because I'm too old for the 'children's room' and too young for the bar. And I like shops full of nice things to look at, and I like amusement arcades and I like boat trips.

Ilfracombe has all kinds of boat trips.

Did I get a boat trip? You must be joking.

I did get a look round a museum, but Maggie can't even go into a museum like an ordinary human being. To be fair, that is an advantage. I can't say I've ever dropped my lolly in excitement at the thought of looking at a lot of worn out bits of things under glass. But Maggie just went in and clonked round on her high heels at a good walking pace, stopping every ten paces to write in her notebook and mutter. 'Victoriana,' she muttered. 'Maps and photos. Stuffed animals. Model ships. Costumes.' I just followed, watching in amazement.

When we came out I said, 'I'm going to send a postcard to Grandma from here, and tell her you won't let me have any fun.'

'Let me know if you need a stamp,' said Maggie, writing something sarcastic about Ilfracombe in her notebook.

I only just had time to buy a card – no time to choose one, you understand, just time to snatch the nearest one from a rack outside a shop and pay for it – and we were on the road for Woolacombe.

Stand back for the high-speed hobos.

Apart from anything else, of course, I was homesick, and homesickness is a funny thing, it spreads without you knowing. I always knew I had been missing Mum and Dad, but once I said that about the postcard I knew I was missing Grandma and Berwick, too.

'Berwick and I could have gone to Grandma's, instead of me down here and him in kennels,' I said. 'Why didn't I think of that? Then I could have visited Mum every day.'

'Grandma couldn't cope with a large dog,' said Maggie.

'What's to cope with? I'd have taken him on walks.'

'There isn't room in her flat. I'm not even sure she's allowed overnight visitors.'

'But who wouldn't allow it? She isn't in a home.'

'It is sheltered accommodation, though,' said Maggie. 'There is a warden and all that. She wouldn't want to get on the wrong side of them. Sheltered flats like that are hard to find.'

'Berwick's never been left before,' I said, 'not since we got him. When Grandma couldn't have him any more, he always went to Linda's.'

I didn't say I wished I could have gone to Linda's. It was too obvious. But all this silly business came up when they were already on their holidays, in the caravan, and no one knew how to get in touch with them.

'Don't worry about Berwick,' said Maggie. 'It's a very good kennels.'

'But he was a stray. His first family abandoned him, and he may think we've done the same thing.'

39

'He won't remember the first time. That was five years ago.'

'Six, and he will remember. You wouldn't forget a trauma like that. Couldn't we have brought him with us?'

'No. Clare, I would have if I could have, but it wouldn't have been fair to either of us.'

'I'd have liked it.'

'I don't mean you and me, I mean me and him. He'd have been stuck in the car all the time, no chance for a good walk, and he might not have been allowed in wherever we stayed.'

I didn't go on about it. I knew it was too late now, and also I knew Maggie would have brought Berwick if she could. She likes him a lot.

'We'll have some lunch in Woolacombe,' said Maggie, 'first thing we do. And then at two o'clock we'll ring the hospital. They'll have everyone tidy for visiting time and there'll probably be someone free to take the phone to her.'

'OK,' I said. 'Yes, thanks. It seems ages since I've spoken to her.'

'It's not really,' said Maggie.

I said, 'I'm hoping they'll let me be there when it's born.'

Maggie looked quickly at me, then she had to look back at the road. 'Are you?' she said. She seemed surprised.

'Yes, but they say they won't. Only Dad. But I have hopes of sneaking in at the last minute, when they're all too busy to notice.'

Maggie didn't say anything for a while. Then she said, 'I think you may find it'll be born by the time we get back.'

'It better hadn't be,' I said. I couldn't quite

40

believe I'd heard her properly. She didn't say anything more.

'It isn't even due till ten days after we get home,' I said.

Still Maggie didn't say anything.

'You think it might be early?' I said. 'You think that's why they've taken her in already? They said it was just because she needs a good rest before it happens – her being an old Mum and all that.'

Maggie was looking unhappy, and I hoped it was just because she's like Dad and doesn't like driving and talking at the same time. 'I don't know that these things are always completely predictable,' she said.

I couldn't tell if she was just having trouble with the Devon signposting or if she was holding out on me. I thought perhaps she was having problems because she didn't know how much I knew about these things. I tried to help her out. 'Is it that you think they might induce it?' I said. 'Is that it?' But then I realized that I really didn't want to hear the answer if it was a 'yes'. 'They couldn't do that,' I said. 'What kind of a home-coming would that be for a baby – Berwick in one place and you and me in another?'

'Well, whatever,' said Maggie. 'We'll be back by the time they come out of hospital.'

'We've got to be back before then,' I said, shocked. 'Dad's all very well, but she's going to want female company, isn't she?'

I looked at Maggie, trying to catch her eye and failing, which I expect was just as well because the roads were quite busy and there were lots of mystery drivers, the sort who don't believe in

41

letting you know which way they're going to turn. 'Do you know something I don't?' I said.

'Why should I?' said Maggie.

'That's not an answer.'

'We'll keep phoning in for bulletins,' said Maggie, 'starting at two o'clock today. And if you're needed, I'll get you back, I promise.'

'I shouldn't have come away.'

'You should, it was helpful. I'll get you back – wherever we are and whatever I have or haven't seen down here, I'll get you back as soon as necessary. OK?'

If Dad can't drive and talk at the same time, then I can't seem to think about two people at the same time. Poor Maggie, she would be worried, too, I'd forgotten that. And she couldn't do more than promise to get me back.

'Yes, OK,' I said. 'That's fine. Thanks.'

At about that time we hit Woolacombe – which was all wind and sand. Well, there was more to it than that, but I was learning that on Maggie-tours you just grasp the obvious and move on. The sand was the most obvious. The place is on a bay, and the sand is flat and yellow and it was full of people – and I knew better than to ask if I could join them. The wind was quite noticeable, too, and it was blowing the sea into shore in peculiarly straight waves – there were wind-surfers riding in on the waves, and their sails were as bright as the beachballs in Ilfracombe had been. The wind was blowing some grey clouds in, too, but we didn't mention those.

Maggie hustled me straight into a little restaurant that smelt of chips and ordered us both a hamburger. Now Woolacombe must have pubs,

42

and hamburgers are not the kind of food you think of when you look at Maggie, so she must have done it for my benefit, and I appreciated that. I don't like hamburgers much either – though they're not so bad if you load on enough relish – but I did appreciate it and I made the best of it.

'They're not really *ham* burgers, you know,' I said to Maggie, as we started on them. 'There isn't any ham in them.'

'I know,' said Maggie, with her mouth full. She hadn't ordered wine for some reason, though House Red and White were on the menu, she'd got a lager.

'They're really cow-lip and eyeball burgers,' I said.

Maggie stopped chewing and looked at me for a moment with her jaws quite still. Then she swallowed hard – quite noisily – and drank a lot of lager. I expect she'd got a gristly bit, you often do.

'Why on earth did you say that?' she said, still staring at me, and looking quite sort of flushed and damp. I wouldn't have thought there was enough alcohol in lager to have that effect, but evidently I was wrong.

'Oh, it's true,' I said, eating mine in smaller mouthfuls and washing it down with Coke. 'There was a programme about it on TV. They use all the worst bits for hamburgers – well, you couldn't use them for anything else, could you? I mean, you can't imagine someone going into a shop and asking for a pound of cow-lip can you?'

Maggie put her hamburger down on her plate and picked up a chip in her fingers and looked at it. She was obviously thinking about what I'd said, which was nice. It gets boring if it's always the adults telling you things — it's nice to tell them things they don't know, for a change.

'Though I don't know why, really,' I said. 'People eat tongue, don't they, and tongue isn't much different from lip, is it? Made of the same stuff, more or less.'

Maggie pushed her plate away, drained her lager glass and signed to the waitress. 'Clare,' she said, 'if you're a vegetarian, I wish you'd just *tell* me.'

'Oh no,' I said. 'I'm not. Well, I am in theory, but I can't keep it up in practice. As Dad says, the spirit is willing but the flesh makes good gravy.'

The waitress came over and Maggie ordered a large black coffee and handed her the plate with the remains of her burger and chips on it.

'Was something wrong?' said the waitress.

'No,' said Maggie. 'I ate a cooked breakfast today and I'm just not used to so much food.'

So she'd taken me to a proper little restaurant when she wasn't even hungry. I was very touched, and I was beginning to feel sorry I'd said the bit about her not having made it.

Chapter Four

Straight after lunch, we rang the hospital, and this time they did take the phone to Mum's bedside. Dad wasn't there – he was going to go in in the evening, she said – but she sounded fine, in fact just as usual. Maggie let me talk first. Just before we went in to the call box I said to her, 'Don't tell me not to ask Mum difficult questions about when it's going to be born. I know better than that.'

And Maggie put her arm round me and gave me an awkward sort of hug and said, 'I'm sure you do.'

So we talked about hospital food – better than you'd expect, she said; and about Dad's job – well he's still got it, she said; and about the other women in the ward – most of them nice, she said. I did ask about the baby, it would have seemed odd not to, but I just said was it still turning cartwheels, and Mum said it was now into double-back-somersaults and she thought someone must have slipped it a yo-yo because more things were kicking her than two fists and two feet. Then we talked about Devon – I said there was a lot of it; and whether I felt car sick – I said not all the time, not at all; and whether we were having good food – I said I was eating more than Maggie.

I can't tell you how often the pips went, they

never seemed to stop, but Maggie had got a lot of change from the restaurant and she had it all stacked up in front of us. Even though I was the one on the phone, she could hear the pips, so she just kept pushing in another coin.

Then she talked to Mum herself, but not for long. She just asked if everything was OK and said she'd ring Dad that night for more detailed news. I was surprised when she hung up because she and Mum usually talk for ages, but she said she was scared to put any more coins in the box in case the weight pulled the whole thing off the wall.

Then she skittered around Woolacombe like a stone skipped across water. I caught up with her each time she stopped to take notes. Then we got in to the car again, and 'Barnstaple, now,' she said.

She's quite a good map reader, Maggie. I think she might even be better than Dad because he often seems to complain that he hasn't got quite the right map, and that some other kind would be better, but Maggie seems to get by on whichever one she heaves out of her cardboard box first. She didn't ask me to map read. I don't know whether it was because she thought I might not be much good at it, or because I'd told her that if I read print for too long in a car I tend to throw up. Anyhow, she took some side roads to Barnstaple so we were back on the narrow stuff again. Narrow, but definitely not straight.

The sky was grey all over by then. It was much cooler without the sun. Soon, rain was coming down in a fine sort of mist, and quite often we had to have the wipers on.

I said, 'What would happen if we met an ambulance on a lane like this?'

'We'd give way, of course,' said Maggie.

'Yes, but suppose we couldn't. Suppose it was on one of those really narrow ones – like we were on yesterday – with only room for one thing at a time. What then?'

'There are passing places for just such an eventuality. I'd reverse into one of those.'

'But suppose you couldn't see one?'

'You have to notice them as you go along. Ideally, I'd know where the nearest one was, and I'd zip back into it.

'But suppose,' I said, 'that what with the ambulance coming on at you, and flashing its light and ringing its bell and all that, you panicked and reversed into the hedge?'

'I'd have to get myself out again, fast.'

'But suppose there was a hidden ditch, and your inside wheels went down in to it and you got completely stuck and couldn't move at all?' I said.

'Clare, I've had an idea,' said Maggie. 'Let's play a game.'

'What game?' I said.

'A fantasy game,' said Maggie. 'Let's pretend you're on my side.'

'What do you mean?' I said.

'Let's pretend you want to help me with my work instead of hinder me. Let's pretend you want to cheer me on instead of trying to hold me back. Let's pretend – if this doesn't sound too far-fetched even for a fantasy game – that we're working *together*.'

I remember that bit clearly. I remember where we were on the road and everything because it

47

was the first time on that trip that I realized that anything I did or said had any effect at all on Maggie. I had thought she was far too distracted to notice me at all. It just goes to show.

'What would I have to do?' I said, very cautiously, because I didn't know at that point if she was pulling my leg or not.

'Thing is,' said Maggie, 'I have to get together a page of jokes for this airline magazine I work for, and I looked in my diary last night for the deadline, and I'll have to get it in the post by the end of this week.'

'*Holiday UK* is an *airline* magazine?'

'No, this is for something different.'

'What – you work for someone else as well?'

'Oh Clare,' said Maggie. 'I work for all sorts of people, I work for who'll pay me, how else am I to "make it" as your father puts it?'

I thought we'd better keep off that. 'What sort of jokes?' I said.

'It's this airline magazine they give away to all the passengers . . .'

'Why is everything you do free?'

' . . . and,' said Maggie, ignoring that, 'I'm supposed to do the children's page. I've done a quiz and a couple of games, and now I need some jokes. The quiz and the games have got animals in them so I thought I might stick with animals – animals going on holiday, perhaps.'

There was a car coming towards us along the narrow lane. It wasn't an ambulance, and there was a passing place in the hedge beside us, so there was no drama. Maggie just pulled over. We watched the car as it edged past us. It had three suitcases strapped to its roof rack, with a bit of

48

black plastic sheeting tied over them – but the wind had torn the plastic so it was hanging in rags. The car looked as it was wearing a very tattered feather hat.

'Luggage,' said Maggie, nodding her head at it. 'It could be "what luggage would different animals take on holiday?" Only don't say "The elephant would pack a trunk", that's too obvious.'

We sat there in silence for a bit. It seemed to me that the whole idea of animals going on holiday was a joke anyway – what more was there to say? But if she really was asking for help with her homework, it seeemed a bit mean to refuse.

I thought about it for a bit, then I said, 'Do you mean like "a horse would pack a nose-bag"?'

'Mm,' said Maggie doubtfully. 'Bit too literal. It really might. More like "a crocodile would pack a handbag".'

'Maggie,' I said, 'aren't you ever afraid this sort of thing will rot your brain?'

'Clare,' said Maggie, speaking through teeth clenched in a deliberately phoney smile, 'if anything's going to rot my brain it'll be your company. I wonder what the technical term is for niece-murder.'

I said, 'Don't bring violence into this, you'll corrupt me.'

'Don't tell me,' said Maggie. 'You saw a TV programme on it.'

'I did, yes. Adults shouldn't take violence for granted, it depraves us young ones.'

'Niece-tricide,' said Maggie, as the other car crept past in slow motion, the driver screwing up his face in fear of clonking his wing mirror. 'Or Natricide, perhaps.'

49

The car finished edging past us and we moved off again. 'OK,' I said. 'I know what luggage a mosquito would pack.'

'What?'

'A gnat-sack.'

'Oho!' said Maggie, putting her foot down a bit. 'That's not too bad. And a camel would pack a sandbag.'

There's a sort of convention at school that you mustn't laugh at each other's jokes, but I did laugh a little, to cheer Maggie up, and then I said, 'Are you doing this just to entertain me?'

'No,' said Maggie. 'I'm working for a living. Some people lay power cables, some people fix teeth, I drive all over the south-west at high speed talking bilge. It's the way it goes. A cat would pack a kit-bag. Open the glove compartment, would you, and see if there's anything to write these down on.'

I opened the little metal door and scrabbled around among the parking meter coins and fluffy unwrapped peppermints and found a pad and a Biro. 'A pig,' I said. 'I know what a pig would pack.'

'You and your pigs. I'll buy it, go on.'

'A pig would pack a porkmanteau!'

Maggie laughed. 'Good, good, write it down. And a gun-dog, write down 'gun-dog'. Get it?'

'No.'

'A gun-dog would pack a shoot-case.'

'All right,' I said, and I've never written so fast in my life. 'A crow!' There was one on the field gate we were passing.

'What then?' said Maggie.

'A crow would pack a carrion-bag,' I said in triumph.

Maggie banged the steering wheel, 'And a mouse would pack a hole-all,' she said, 'and a cow would take a moo-sic case.'

'I can't write so fast,' I said.

'You're not going to throw up?' said Maggie.

'No, it's just that I'll never read this back. Wait! I've got the last word. What would a gorilla pack?'

And we both answered in chorus, 'Anything it blooming well liked.'

And that was how we hit Barnstaple in the first good humour of the trip.

Maggie even explained to me a bit more about what she was doing. I mean, I started the conversation, but she needn't have followed it up. I said, 'Right, now I'm working with you, can I say something about the way you work?'

'Go ahead,' said Maggie.

'Well – if you're going to write a really good piece about Devon, like you did about London . . .'

'You've read it?' said Maggie.

'No, I haven't read it, but I saw it.'

'Oh,' said Maggie.

'Well – I mean, shouldn't you take your time? Really to do it properly, shouldn't you spend a long time in each place, see it in all weathers, talk to the local people, get the feel of it? Isn't that what real writers do? Wouldn't it all come out better in the end?'

Maggie was just parking when I said that, and instead of getting out right away, she sat there for a few minutes, playing with the ignition keys. I think it was partly because neither of us was keen to get out in the rain.

51

'The short answer,' said Maggie, 'is that for this kind of job you only get paid a set amount of money, and you get given a set deadline. Now, if you spend longer on it than the deadline allows, two things happen. The first is that you're out of pocket, because what should have been one week's money gets stretched out to cover two, or three, or however long you take. And the second is that you're out of work because they mark you down as unreliable, and don't use you again. Does that make sense?'

'Kind of,' I said. 'But shouldn't they pay you enough in the first place so you don't have to do it so fast?'

'They have their profit margins to consider. This *Holiday UK* – it makes its money by selling advertising, right? Well it's new, so the advertisers can't know for sure how many people are going to read it, so it can't charge too much per advert. Because they just wouldn't pay. So from what it knows it's getting from advertising, it works out what it can spend on paper, and printing, and distribution, and office staff, and other writers – and me. And while it's working out those sums it always bears in mind what it wants to keep back for profit.'

I thought about that, then I said, 'What if you told it you just wouldn't work for it unless it paid you more?'

'Then it would find someone else.'

'It wouldn't pay more to keep you?'

Maggie dropped her keys into her bag and then turned and grinned at me. 'No,' she said. 'No, it wouldn't.'

'But Maggie – aren't you special?'

'Oh yes,' said Maggie. 'I am. But very few people know it. It's just the way things are, Clare. It all comes down to money.'

And not long after that, in the heart of Barnstaple, it did.

Barnstaple, by the way, is a port and a bridge and a shopping centre with a craft market. It doesn't have a cinema, and it wouldn't have been any use to me if it had. Normal people on holiday on a wet afternoon would head straight for somewhere that had. Me, I just put my anorak hood up and thought how good I was being about everything.

There was a Tourist Information Centre in a caravan at the edge of our park, so we dashed in there and snatched up some leaflets. Flicking through the leaflets I discovered something I wished I hadn't because it was much harder to be good about it than about the cinema.

'Lundy, Maggie!' I said. 'You can get to Lundy from here.'

'It would take a whole day,' said Maggie – rather like someone else might have said 'it would take a whole year'.

'I know, but look, you sail on a ship called *The Polar Bear* and you land on something called Rat Island.'

'You need to book,' said Maggie, 'and we haven't.'

'But it would be so exciting – they might be able to fit us in. Think of sailing right off to an island in the middle of the sea. There are bound to be caves there, and look, there are birds – aren't you supposed to know about bird-watching places?'

'I do know about them,' said Maggie. 'I've picked up the same leaflet as you have. Clare, it's *raining*.'

'I know.'

'It wouldn't be nice in the rain – even if we had the time, and even if we were booked on the boat, it wouldn't be any fun in the rain.'

'I'm English,' I said. 'I can have fun in the rain.'

Maggie was scrabbling through the leaflets and I thought it was just because she didn't want to miss a moment getting on with her research, but then she stopped scrabbling and began to read aloud. 'Rat Island,' she said, 'is one of the last outposts of the Black Rat, *Rattus Rattus*.'

'You were looking for something to put me off,' I said. 'You failed – I like rats.'

'And,' read Maggie, 'it is also home to the trapdoor spider.'

Maggie knows me better than I thought.

'You're right,' I said. 'Lundy wouldn't be fun in the rain.'

Barnstaple wasn't much fun in the rain, either, but that's what we were stuck with. Buildings and shops. It's not terrific looking at things when your anorak hood is dripping on your trainers and when bits of rain settle on your eyelashes so that everything looks as if it's inside an aquarium tank.

Then Maggie stopped in our lightning tour outside a bank. It was shut, because it was pushing five o'clock by then. So she shoved one of her plastic cards into the cash dispenser and tapped out her number. She didn't find it easy because she was trying to balance her umbrella on her shoulder, and to hold her bag, open and full of stuff, on one arm, while she took the card in and out of it. Mum would have given me either the bag or the umbrella to hold. Maggie didn't think of that. You can tell she's used to doing things on her own.

She got the card back, and a piece of paper, and then she rested her forehead against the wall for a moment, in mock agony.

At least, I think it was mock.

'What's the matter?' I said.

'I've just had a rejection slip from this wall,' said Maggie. 'It won't give me any money.'

'Why not?'

'Well, basically because there isn't any in my account.'

That gave me a real fright. I've never been away from home without money before – unless I was with Dad and Mum and their money. I knew it was actually very important. The thing is, you can't eat in restaurants, or sleep in hotels, without it – not that we were booked in anywhere, needless to say.

'Haven't you got *any* cash?' I said cautiously.

'No,' said Maggie. Then she patted the hood of my anorak lightly, the way she does to Berwick's head, and said, 'Don't worry, I'll see you OK. Just let me get used to the idea.'

And she never said, never once, a single word about all those coins she'd stuffed in to the telephone box when I was talking to Mum. Even at the time I'd only noticed because it was a nuisance when the pips kept on interrupting, but Maggie must have known then how much she was spending. I didn't want to spoil it by thanking her for not saying it, so by way of return I didn't ask her what we were going to do, and where we were going to stay, and stuff like that.

She did appreciate it. As we walked away from the bank she put her arm around me, the way Mum does but the way Maggie generally doesn't, and said, 'Thank you for not asking me why I didn't know my account was empty.'

That wasn't what I hadn't asked, if you understand me, but I *was* deliberately not asking questions, so I took the credit.

'Anyway,' said Maggie, 'you have a right to know. I'm overdue for the London-piece money. He said he'd pay it directly into the account – I left him the number and everything – but . . . he hasn't.'

'Who's "he"?' It seemed OK to ask that in the circumstances.

'"He" is *Holiday UK* – although his mother knows him as Nigel Kellie. He founded the magazine and launched it. He's quite good at launching things. Launching and lunching, those are his true talents. He does them both quite often. Unkind people would say he has to, because his projects tend to fall by the wayside, so he has to keep on launching new ones. Usually over lunch.'

'What would kind people say?'

'Oh that he has a lot of bad luck but perseveres anyway. But the most important thing to know about him is that he has an allergy, a really terrible allergy.'

Maggie seemed quite wound up about it, and I didn't really want to interrupt, but I couldn't help saying, 'What kind of allergy?'

56

'He's allergic,' said Maggie, 'to signing cheques.'

'Oh,' I said. 'Maggie, I've got some cash. If we can just stop walking for a moment, I can count it.'

'No need,' said Maggie. 'Although I do appreciate the offer. When the bank is actually open tomorrow I'll be able to do some negotiating. In the meantime, I think we'd better decide to stay in Barnstaple tonight. It's no good going to a cheap Bed and Breakfast place because they'll want cash. We're going to have to stay somewhere big enough to take credit cards. The MONEY that man costs me.'

'But Dad says that paying by credit card is just deferring the problem,' I said.

'My whole life is spent deferring problems,' said Maggie. 'Keep your eyes skinned for a Visa or Access sign. We don't run to American Express in this family.'

Chapter Five

Well of course it just wasn't that easy to walk
into a credit card hotel. People who travel on spec
tend to go to the cheaper places – which want
cash. People who plan on going to real hotels,
even small ones, tend to book their rooms in
advance. When we were turned down in the third
hotel, by an indignant receptionist who kept
glaring at my shoes, I said that perhaps we
should try some other place, but Maggie said this
was the biggest town in the area and so the most
likely bet.

Behind the counter in the lobby of the fourth
hotel there was quite an old man with black hair
that was turning white and a black moustache
that was going the same way. There was a
cigarette burning in an ashtray on the counter,
but I could see that usually he held it in his
mouth as he worked because there was a yellow
stain on one side of his moustache and a fainter
one on the white bits of hair above it. It gave him
odd markings, a bit like a cat down our street.

He said no, sorry, they were fully booked, and
then he looked at me and changed his mind. The
thing was that when he said they were full, as
well, I suddenly got a feeling of real panic and I
couldn't begin to imagine what would become of

us. I mean the 'no money' thing had given me a fright, but this was real fear. I didn't say anything, and I certainly didn't cry, but he must have noticed something in my expression because he said, 'If you're really stuck there is one room I could let you have. But it's not really very suitable.'

'In what way?' said Maggie.

Anyone else might have thought that Maggie, at least, was perfectly calm, but I'd noticed that she kept hauling her mac belt more tightly round her, as if she was going to cut herself in half with it. Also, as we waited at one reception desk after another, she kept tapping one of her wet feet in its strappy red sandal. Of course, now that I think about it, that may not have been tension, that may have been because she thought that if she kept her foot moving no one would notice that the dye from the shoe was beginning to come off on it.

'It's a children's room,' he said, 'with two bunk beds. Very small, no TV.'

'We'll take it,' said Maggie. 'I'd rather have my feet hanging out over the edge of a bunk than take them out in the rain again.'

'They're full-sized bunks,' he said. 'Your feet won't hang over. Come up and look at it before you decide.'

We had decided – but we trotted up with him and reassured him that it was fine. It *was* fine. It was small, like a cabin, but it had its own washbasin, and a tiny bedside locker with a light on it. In fact it had more furniture than that big farmhouse bedroom. Outside, on a bit of flat roof, there was a kind of shed thing, with a generator humming away inside it.

'Does that go on all night?' said Maggie.

'Afraid so,' he said. 'If you want to reconsider, you're not committed . . .' He seemed a very kind man.

'Fear not,' said Maggie. 'We'll get our stuff in now.'

Because we were so damp we decided to have baths and change and then Maggie said she'd take us out to dinner because the hotel dining room looked claustrophobic to her. Anyway, being only a small hotel, they served dinner too early for her – seven o'clock or something. You might think that the robotic hens' eggs and the cowlip burger would have kept me going, but all the rushing around and worrying about money had given me an appetite.

'We could eat here,' I said hopefully. 'Early. It'd save having to go out in the rain again.'

'We'll go in the car,' said Maggie. 'It'll be all right. And can you wear a dress – or at least a skirt and not jeans? Don't forget, we can't afford to go anywhere cheap.'

'Just as well,' I said. 'I'm running out of socks.'

'What do you mean?'

'These are wet.'

'But haven't you any others?'

'Yes, but I wear clean ones every day,' I said, 'and what I've got won't last the week. Who's going to wash them – you or me?'

'Oh Clare!' said Maggie, and she seemed really upset. 'I hadn't even *thought* about washing. I can't! We don't stay anywhere long enough to get them dry again. Why on earth couldn't you have counted the days and brought enough?'

'I did – originally.'

'What went wrong, then?'

'Oh,' I said, 'it's a long story and it has a spider in it. You wouldn't want to know.'

'I have to tell you,' said Maggie, and she was only half joking, 'that I didn't bargain for you giving your underwear away to every stray insect you took a fancy to. Did you have to give it four pairs? Don't answer that. I think I'd rather buy you sandals, so you don't need socks.'

'No thanks,' I said. There are some things that can't be changed. 'I always wear trainers. Except with a skirt.'

'So I noticed. Don't your feet get very sweaty in this warm weather?'

'Yes, that's why I need clean socks every day.'

'I'm tempted,' said Maggie, 'to suggest cutting off your feet, but I suppose you'd accuse me of gratuitous violence.'

'I would if I could pronounce the word you said before "violence".'

Before we went out for dinner, Maggie tried to get hold of Dad, but it was the usual thing. First, lines to London were engaged. Then, she found she'd missed him at the hospital and he wasn't at home either. She said she thought he might have gone back to the office from the hospital. I said I thought that might be overdoing things a bit, but she said he was closely involved in smoothing the path of the merger – it would be bound to involve him in a lot of work, even if he wasn't also trying to create a good impression. Anyhow, she left our number with the night sister again. I could see, now, that that didn't have to mean we were all expecting some terrible drama. It was just the sensible thing to do as we were on the move all

the time. Anyway, I'd had my talk with Mum
that morning, so I felt fine. It seemed more
important to talk to Mum – who was just lying
there – than to Dad, who was busy anyway.

Then Maggie rang Nigel Kellie. The phone
was in the main foyer, and there wasn't a
proper box, just one of those half-globe things
you stick your head in, so it wasn't exactly
private. She tried to keep her voice down, but
odd words kept drifting up the well of the stairs
to our attic room, where I lay on the top bunk,
flicking through some of the guidebooks she'd
brought with us.

I'd offered her some of my change – I did owe
it to her, after all – but she said she'd take great
pleasure in reversing the charges. I hope she
did, because I don't think she took much pleasure in the conversation. I could hear that she
kept trying to get to the problem about the
London money, but he was obviously keen to
talk about other things.

'But there's nothing *in* the middle,' she said,
several times. 'It doesn't make sense. There's
the north coast and there's the south coast and
there's Dartmoor, and that's all.' Then later she
said, 'Well, but there can't be pixies *every*where.'
Then she said. 'Yes, but you promised before –
will you definitely pay it in this time?' Then,
'But to get back to the London money – apart
from the fact that it's mine, it isn't only me
who's suffering, I'm a one-parent family for a
week.' Then she went back to the bit about
there being nothing in the middle, and the
whole thing seemed to start all over again.

When she came back up to the room she was

all flustered and cross, and I kept quiet. We set out to find dinner in silence.

In the car she started talking, but to herself rather than to me. 'It's all very well,' she said, yanking the gear lever to and fro, much harder than usual, as we cruised around the streets of Barnstaple, 'but you do the work on time – that's vital – oh yes, that's essential – and then they muck about and muck about and don't part with the money – and it's *my* money – so I run up credit card bills – *and* what about the interest I'm paying on those – and then he maunders on about wanting a page on The Middle. And I tell him there's nothing *in* The Middle. And he just smiles – you can actually hear him smiling and twinkling down the telephone line, you know – and he says, "Don't be so negative, Mags, go and find something." And I try to say that I actually do *need* to see Clovelly, and then get on to Dartmoor as fast as possible, and he just smiles and twinkles and pours himself a Scotch, gloop, gloop it goes over the wires, you can almost smell it – and then he says that my trouble is that I worry too much about money. But still he doesn't pay in *my* money – *and* he doesn't listen to a word I say . . .'

'Are we going to Dartmoor?' I said, when she paused for a bit. 'Isn't that where *The Hound of the Baskervilles* came from?'

'Oh God,' said Maggie, 'that's *all* I need, a gigantic hound.' Then she sort of pawed the air in my direction with one hand and said, 'Sorry, sorry, it isn't your fault. Yes, it is where *The Hound of the Baskervilles* came from. I'll tell you the story sometime. Meanwhile, it's very appropriate to talk

63

about hounds because talking to Nigel always gives me a black dog on my shoulder.'

'What does that mean?'

'Puts me in a bad mood.'

'Why a black dog? Berwick's a black dog, and he wouldn't put anyone in a bad mood.'

'Dear Berwick,' said Maggie, absently. 'I think it's because black dogs are associated with the devil in some legends.'

'Nothing in the middle of what?' I said.

'Devon,' said Maggie. 'There's nothing in the middle of Devon. There's this area called mid-Devon and there isn't anything in it, but we have to go and find it anyway, OK?'

'And miss out Clovelly?'

'No, we can't do that. We'll have to do a dawn raid on Clovelly tomorrow — and then belt off into nothingness.'

'There must be *something* there,' I said. 'I mean, I'm not siding with Nasty Nigel or anything, but there must be *something*.'

'Oh — yes — there's lots. There's farms and villages and people living their lives. But there's nothing really for tourists. Hardly any restaurants, no museums, no steam railway rides — just nice walks for hikers, and hikers don't buy magazines like *Holiday UK*.'

'But we have to go?'

'But we have to go.'

Maggie drew in and parked outside a nice-looking restaurant. 'This is in one of the guides,' she said. 'I think it sounds OK. Let's try it. And I'm afraid we'll have to make an early start tomorrow, because if we're going to fit in miles of unnecessary farm lanes as well as everything else, we're going to have to move a bit faster than we have up to now.'

I didn't say anything, I promise I didn't, but I did look at her, and she looked at me, and then we both began to laugh at the same time.

'You're like the Red Queen in *Alice Through the Looking Glass*,' I said. 'Faster! Faster! No wonder you wear red shoes.'

'The Wicked Witch of the North wore red shoes, too, so watch yourself,' said Maggie.

I said, 'I bet the dye didn't dare come off on *her* feet.'

'Let's please keep off the subject of feet,' said Maggie. 'Yours, the spider's and mine.'

So we went in to the restaurant, which was very pretty, with candles and flowers on the tables, and a sweet trolley, and a smartly dressed waiter.

'Make the most of this,' Maggie whispered in my ear as he led us to a table. 'If my money comes through tomorrow, we won't be able to afford to eat like this again.'

We sat down and she took the menu he gave her and said to him, 'Before I look at this, could I order half a bottle of the House Red, as a matter of extreme urgency.'

When he'd gone off, smiling, she looked at me over the menu and said, 'I want you to know I would never, ever, ask you to lie to your father.'

'But you don't want me to tell him you haven't got any money?'

'If he asks,' said Maggie, 'tell him the truth. But just don't force the information on him.'

'Well he isn't likely to ask, is he?' I said.

'Nope,' said Maggie. Then she read the menu. I was facing her so I couldn't see it, I could just

65

see the names of fancy wines on the back, but I could see her face – and her smile just spread and spread.

'That good, huh?' I said.

'So good,' said Maggie, 'that I'm going to order for you, too.'

And when the waiter came back, very quickly, with a jug-thing of wine and a glass she said, with a sort of triumph in her voice, 'Two Vegetarian Specials, please. Oh, and what do you want to drink, Clare?'

I had Perrier Water. I think it tastes like soda water poured over old bed springs, but that place was too classy for Coke.

As the waiter went away, Maggie leant forward to me and said, 'I think I'm beginning to learn how to eat in your company. But just please don't tell me about some TV programme that said that all vegetables are full of pesticides and poisonous fertilizers, OK?'

'I couldn't anyway,' I said. 'I missed that one.'

There were only four other people in the restaurant when we got there, two couples, but I could see more were expected because there were two tables pushed together and laid up nicely for eight, flowers and candles in the middle, and everything. The eight arrived before our food did, eight men, all about Dad's age, talking loudly and kind of banging about as they got themselves sitting down, so that the calm feeling that had been there somehow wasn't there any more.

'Car salesmen?' said Maggie quietly to the waiter, as he brought our Vegetarian Specials.

'Businessmen's convention,' said the waiter.

'Three day event. They were here last night and the night before, too.'

That was all he said, and he didn't have any particular expression on his face when he said it, but I got the distinct feeling that he was telling us he'd be glad when it was tomorrow night.

'These jokes,' said Maggie, as we began to eat. 'I was thinking about them in the bath and I wondered if we could go on from the luggage to something about the kind of holiday different animals would take.'

'Aha!' I said. 'We're having our own business convention. A working dinner.'

'Exactly so,' said Maggie.

There was a roar of laughter from the men in their suits around their table, which was just across from us; but when I looked over I could see they weren't laughing at anything we'd said, they couldn't hear us, they were passing two bottles of wine round the table in opposite directions, and some of them seemed to be taking wine out of each bottle. The waiter was standing patiently by, with his pad, waiting to take their order for food.

'Right,' I said, sipping my Perrier, and wishing sophisticated drinks tasted nicer, 'What have you got so far?'

Maggie tipped herself over sideways and scraped around in her bag on the floor for her notebook. 'I started,' she said, 'with "a stoat would go somewhere wease-ly reached, whereas a weasel would go somewhere stoat-ally different." But I really wanted something a bit simpler than that.'

We began too giggle. 'You think that's too intellectual?' I said.

'Too involved,' said Maggie. 'I want shorter things, really. Like – well, like "a wolf would go fang-gliding".'

'My pig,' I said, 'would go ham-gliding.'

'I prefer that,' said Maggie, and she put her notebook beside the plate and wrote it down.

The waiter appeared beside us just as I said, 'Do you think a kangaroo would go island-hopping?'

'I'm sure of it,' said Maggie, 'and a leopard would try out various nice spots.' She turned to the waiter, who looked a bit dazed, I thought. 'Sorry,' she said, and waited for what he wanted to say.

'The gentlemen at the table over there,' said the waiter – and without looking round I could tell that their table had gone quiet – 'are asking if you would care to join them. You and your sister.'

Maggie looked over at the other table, so I did, too. Seven of them were looking back at us, their faces all red and shiny in the candlelight, and one raised his wine glass to Maggie. At once, the others did the same. The eighth man, who was slowly stirring his soup but not drinking it, didn't look up. I thought he looked embarrassed.

Maggie replied to the waiter, but her voice was clear enough to carry across to the business convention. 'No thank you,' she said. 'Please tell them we're very comfortable here.' And she smiled at me, and drank some wine, and didn't look at the waiter or the other table again. The waiter smiled, and nodded, and turned away.

'How did you do that?' I said admiringly.

'Do what?'

'Well you only said "no", but you made it sound as if you'd turn them all to stone if they asked again.'

'Did I? Oh good,' said Maggie. She leant forward and I thought she was going to tell me something very important about turning down invitations from strange men, but what she actually said was, 'A sheep would go on a baa-crawl.'

'A hare,' I said, 'would go mad.'

'But only in March,' said Maggie. 'And a cow would tour the moo-seums.'

We stared at each other, glassy-eyed, as our brains chased around for something else. Maggie beat me. 'A horse,' she said, slowly, 'would stay near home and visit neigh-bours.'

There was another roar of laughter from the other table, but it was nothing to do with us. Their voices were getting louder and louder, and when they shouted for more wine I could hear exactly what they ordered.

'Next to them, you look sober,' I said to Maggie.

For some reason she looked really cross for a moment. 'I am sober,' she said. 'You've never seen me any other way.'

'Well you know what I mean,' I said.

The waiter reappeared to gather up our plates just as Maggie got rid of her frown and leant forward to say to me, 'Elephants would take Bun-day off and puppies would take Chews-day.'

I said, 'I worry about you.'

'Will there be anything else?' said the waiter, who had a really nice smiley face.

'Yes,' said Maggie. 'Chickens would take

69

Hens-day off. And I would like some coffee and I think my guest would like a pudding.'

'Can I?' I said.

'I'm sure *Nigel*'s having a pudding,' said Maggie. 'So why not us?'

'You're not?'

'I'm full. Eat one for me.'

The waiter pulled this trolley of stuff over and parked it beside me, and I didn't know what to do first. I wanted to choose something to eat, but I wanted to get the next day before Maggie. I counted quickly on my fingers, 'Bun-day, Chews-day, Hens-day – yes a cat would take Furs-day off.'

'And what will the young lady take?' said the waiter, who was chuckling to himself. Some people would have taken a "that's neither clever nor funny" line, but I suppose he was used to being patient with loonies like us.

I chose a chocolate meringue thing, and while he was spooning it out I said to Maggie, 'My pig would take Sty-day off.'

'And rabbits would take Salad-day,' said Maggie.

The waiter gave me my plate and stepped back a couple of paces, but he didn't go, he hung around to catch the end of the week.

Maggie poured herself a second glass of wine. 'I can hear your brain ticking,' she said.

I said, 'You've got the last one, I can tell.'

'Try,' said Maggie.

'I am.'

'Bees . . . ' said Maggie.

And we shouted together, 'Would take a Hon-day.'

The waiter nodded to himself and wheeled the trolley to the back of the restaurant, where he'd got it from.

There was another great roar from the other table, much louder than our little shout, and I looked round. 'Maggie!' I said.

Maggie was looking down at her notebook, writing. The waiter reappeared and put a cup of coffee by her elbow. 'Thanks,' said Maggie. Then, to me, 'I've got something on the go here, but I haven't quite worked it out yet.'

'Maggie! They're pouring *wine* over each other.'

'I'm not at all surprised,' said Maggie, and she still didn't look up.

Well you can't be expected not to watch something like that, and they weren't taking any notice of me, so I just stared. That's why I saw the eighth man get up quietly and put his napkin down and go to the back of the restaurant where the waiter was. He talked to him for a moment, and gave him some money, and then he turned towards the door, leaving. As he got to our table he stopped for a moment, and Maggie sensed him there, and looked up. 'It looks *much* more fun at your table,' he said, and nodded, and smiled, and left. Maggie smiled back, one of her real ones, not one of her frozen ones, and as the door closed behind him I said, 'He seemed nice.'

'I think he was nice,' said Maggie. 'That's why he didn't ask us to join them.'

'Don't nice ones ever ask you to join them?'

'Not when they're married.'

'How could you tell?'

71

'Wedding ring,' said Maggie. 'They've all got them, not that it seems to make much difference. Eight of them, and only one grown-up.' She made writing signs in the air to the waiter, and he nodded, and began to make out our bill. 'Let's not get morbid,' said Maggie. 'Now brace yourself, I'm ready, and this is my *pièce de résistance*. OK?'

'OK.'

The waiter came nearer, with his bill pad.

'Right,' said Maggie. 'A donkey would take a bray off but a dog would only go for arf a day. A mouse would take a full squeak. A pig would go for a porknight. A cow would travel midden week. A cat would take Spring Bank Holiday, and a kangaroo would only go in Leap Year. A hedgehog would take flea weeks – a monkey would take paw weeks – and a three-toed sloth would take a lo-o-o-o-ong vague-ation.'

'If I can write that down for my daughter,' said the waiter closing in, 'the chocolate meringue is on the house.'

'Go ahead,' said Maggie, and pushed her notebook over to him.

I felt a bit guilty. I whispered to Maggie, while he wrote on his pad in his neat waiter's shorthand, 'You've done the work and I get the wages.'

Maggie winked at me. 'I don't mind which of us gets them,' she said, 'as long as one of us does. Do you realize that's the first work I've done in the last four weeks that I've actually been paid for. It's very satisfying. And now let's pay and get out before the business convention gets travel sick.'

'You can't get travel sick in a stationary room,' I said.

'I very much doubt if they think this room is stationary,' said Maggie, selecting a credit card.

Chapter Six

When we got back to the hotel, Maggie went straight in to the little bar off the lobby, and then came straight back out again.

'Who was in there?' I said, as we went upstairs.

'No one,' said Maggie.

'Who were you looking for?'

'No one,' said Maggie. 'I mean I was positively looking for no one, I was hoping no one would be there.'

'Why?'

Maggie unlocked the door of our room and chucked her mac on the bottom bunk. 'Because I'm going down there to write up my notes,' she said, 'while you put the light out and get off to sleep.'

'Well that's a *really* friendly end to an evening,' I said.

'You don't mind?' said Maggie, looking startled. 'I'll only be downstairs.'

I was learning Maggie's startled look. Sometimes it came because she was surprised at something, sometimes she put it on deliberately to show me she thought I was being unreasonable.

'*I* don't mind if *you* don't,' I said. 'If *you* don't care that your liver will get all swollen and mushy, why should I?'

'Oh God,' said Maggie.

'It's true,' I said. 'I saw a programme about it on TV.'

'You watch altogether too much TV,' said Maggie.

'I only watch serious stuff,' I said. 'Educational.'

'Well I think you ought to try and take in some trash from time to time,' said Maggie, 'and make all our lives easier.'

And she went off and left me in the little cabin-like room. I went to bed in the bottom bunk and pretended I was in a boat and that the hum from the generator outside was the hum of the engine. I wanted to stay awake until Maggie came back, but it wasn't easy. The bed was comfortable, the pillow fitted itself around my head just right, and the box outside hummed an electrical lullaby. I kept drifting off into those half-dreams where you think your arm has peacefully separated itself from the rest of you, and where your feet are so relaxed they feel as if they might be on back to front. I was floating around like that, half believing I was coming to pieces and thinking how nice it felt, when I was woken by the glow of the landing light. It came into the room with Maggie and then vanished as she closed the door behind her.

'I'm in the bottom bunk,' I said out of the darkness.

'So I hear,' said Maggie. 'Why? I thought you'd chosen the top one.'

'I was too tired to climb up.'

'What you really mean is you wanted to make me climb up.'

I could hear the rustling as she undressed. Then I heard her bare feet making faint sticky sounds on the rungs of the little metal ladder that led to the top bunk. The pale glow from the window – we hadn't drawn the curtains – showed Maggie's legs moving alternately upwards. As they went out of sight there was a nasty hard noise – shin bone on metal – and Maggie's voice saying something very quiet and very fierce that I didn't quite catch.

'I expect people who sleep in top bunks,' I said, 'don't usually drink two bottles of wine before trying to get into them.'

'You have a very inflated idea of my capacity,' said Maggie, and the entire framework shook as she lay down.

'Maggie?' I said.

'Mm?'

'Before we went out, when you were talking to Nutty Nigel on the phone – what did you mean when you said, "There can't be pixies *every*where"?

'Oh,' said Maggie. She yawned loudly and turned over. 'Michael's having a hard time in Cornwall.'

'Who's Michael?'

'He's my Cornish counterpart. Apparently he's got writer's block, sightsee-er's eyes, walker's foot and driver's sickness. Finally, he's being pixie-led.'

'What does that mean?'

'They say the pixies come out at night with lanterns, especially on moors and bleak places, and lead lost travellers into marshes and mires where they get even more lost – and probably drown.'

'I thought pixies were supposed to be lucky, I didn't know they were evil.'

'They're not really evil. They just have a dubious sense of humour.'

'Sounds evil to me. Do you mean this Michael's seeing real ones?'

'Oh no, I don't think so. I'm exaggerating. He's

76

just being bedevilled by plastic ones and plaster ones and stone ones and postcard ones. The Cornish have a thing about pixies and it seems he can't shake them off.'

'Sounds more like a pixie stake-out,' I said. 'So you mean he's doing what you're doing?'

'Yup.'

'I didn't realize there were others like you.'

'There are three counties in the West Country issue. There's us doddering around Devon, Carole staggering all over Somerset, and Michael careering up and down Cornwall. As a matter of fact – if we didn't have to go off to mid-Devon I was going to call in at a Gnome Sanctuary not far from here. I could have sent him a postcard. I wouldn't want him to think he's the only one who's suffering.'

'Gnomes aren't pixies.'

'These gnomes have pixies in their reserve with them. Good night. My mushy liver and I need our sleep.'

'So Devon has pixies, too?'

'You wait,' said Maggie, and yawned again, 'until Dartmoor. That's got things to knock pixies into a pointed hat. Headless horsemen, a phantom woman in a carriage made of bone, and the Devil hunting with his pack of red-eyed Wisht hounds. Sweet dreams, Clare. And if you have a nightmare don't hesitate to let me sleep through it.'

I didn't dream at all, I don't think. My arms and legs drifted off again, and I followed them, and nothing nasty happened to us while we were away.

The only problem was that the night didn't last

long enough. Maggie had us out of our bunks not much after dawn, and she didn't even wait till I'd washed to tell me we'd be getting breakfast on the road. The sun was shining, but we had learnt the weather by then, we knew it would quite likely rain by the afternoon, so we didn't get over-excited.

I did get vaguely excited when I decided we might be doing a flit. Maggie said she'd settled up the night before, but she was so desperate to get us out of the place – got quite manic when I actually wanted to choose what to wear instead of just putting on the first thing – that I couldn't help being a bit suspicious.

When she said we'd better go down the stairs quietly so as not to wake the other guests, I was almost sure. Then as we reached the lobby I saw that someone was standing in the open hotel doorway, with his back to us, and as Maggie didn't hesitate or hold back, I guessed I was wrong. It was the old man with the cat moustache, standing on the steps smoking a cigarette. He looked as though he was trying to set up a smoke screen in the porch so that the air that went in to the lobby would be filtered through it. Straight air with no smoke in it would probably kill him.

Anyway, he told us it was a nice day, as if him saying it made it official, and he also told us to have a nice trip. He obviously wouldn't have said any of that if we'd just ripped him off. I didn't tell Maggie what I'd thought. I had understood that money definitely wasn't her best subject.

When we started out all I cared about was that I'd had no breakfast. When we really got under

78

way, my main problem was that we seemed to be covering even more ground than before so that it took three packs of extra-strong mints to keep the nausea at bay. (Don't believe anyone who tells you it isn't possible to feel sick and hungry at the same time. It's very easy.)

I didn't know then that mid-Devon had it in for me – or that there was a frightening piece of information waiting at our next overnight stop. Looking back, of course, I can see that it wasn't really like that. The news wasn't lying in ambush for me. It was at the hospital, and it just happened to make contact with me that evening. It wasn't the fault of the place. Even so, I'll always connect it with that bit of Devon where Maggie said there was Nothing.

But for most of the main part of the day I was thinking about my stomach, one way or another.

We drove to Appledore, which is on a rather complicated river estuary, and whose name made me fantasize about Cox's Orange Pippins. I asked Maggie what its password was, and she said 'shipyard'. The yard was a big one, but though you'd expect people to begin building ships early in the day we were too early even for them, and the huge covered yard was quite silent. 'I expect they're all having breakfast,' I said hopefully to Maggie. She didn't take the hint. Down at the waterfront they were bringing in a fishing trawler with a slithery silver catch. Maggie took photos, but I walked on by. I was afraid some of them might be still alive and I don't like to see them drowning in air. Apart from feeling sorry for them, the whole idea is so weird.

We could see right out to the mouth of the

estuary and Maggie said there was a sandbank under the water, like a kind of natural booby trap for ships. She said it was called the Bideford Bar. I asked if it served bar snacks, but she ignored me. Then she pointed out the sand dunes on each side of the estuary mouth. She said one heap of dunes was a country park and the other was a nature reserve — and both of them had golf courses on them. I thought that was extraordinary, as though golfers were an endangered species or something. And what if one of them mistook a bird's egg for the ball and scrambled it into the hole? I didn't say that, I knew she wasn't really talking to me, she was just saying her notes out loud as she wrote them. I did say, though, that from this distance the dunes looked the same colour as digestive biscuits.

We couldn't do much in Appledore because the museum was closed as well as the yard, so we went on to Westward Ho! You should have seen what happened when Maggie met Westward Ho! It was a bit like Dracula seeing a silver cross. Pleating the sides of her mouth wasn't enough, she drew in her breath in a kind of hiss, too, and curled her left nostril. It's fun, you see, that's the problem with it as far as she's concerned. It's a great big smashing holiday camp with amusement arcades and a riding school and something — according to a signboard — called the Tyrolean Beer Gardens with an ice-skating rink and everything. There were people around but it was still a bit early, so it was really quite quiet. I asked Maggie if she was going to take a photo, but she just snorted and said that what she was going to do was drive to Bideford as fast as possible.

'I bet they do good breakfasts somewhere here,' I said.

But Maggie just nudged me back into the car saying, 'For a thin child, you have a remarkable obsession with food.'

It was a very short run from there to Bideford, but there was quite a lot of traffic. I found the blue, red and green cars made me think of Penguin biscuits. Most of the delivery trucks were advertising food anyway. There were yoghurts and bread, and a tanker of milk and a truckful of cauliflowers, all heading for absolutely anywhere except my stomach. When a two-tone beige and cream dormobile overtook us, I couldn't help pointing out to Maggie that it was very like Mum's soup flask. But all Maggie said was, 'The wheels on the dormobile are bigger.'

I began to wonder if this was what Maggie had meant by getting breakfast on the road – just looking at traffic and fantasizing. Then I remembered. Of course. We didn't have any money.

'I'll buy us breakfast in Bideford,' I said. I enjoyed saying it. It made me feel I was in charge for once.

Maggie looked a bit flustered. 'If we hang around in Bideford until half past nine,' she said, 'when the banks open, I can persuade them to call my London branch and let me take out some money.'

'What's Bideford?' I said.

'It's a 24-arch bridge, a port which now only deals in pleasure trips, a market, a shopping centre, cinema and art gallery.'

'OK,' I said. 'Well the last lot won't be open yet. You're never going to let us have a pleasure trip

81

– UGH, PLEASURE, Ptah! And it'll only take you three minutes to photograph the bridge. So let me buy us breakfast there and we can get on to Clovelly – otherwise this dawn raid is going to run into midnight.'

'We can eat further along the way, after nine thirty.'

'That'll be lunch. Maggie, I'm desperate. The road is beginning to look like a stick of liquorice, the houses look like iced biscuits, the sun is a poached egg. Even you're beginning to look good. What'll Mum say if you drive me to cannibalism?'

There was a nice big cafe on the quayside, posh enough for Maggie, and we had a full breakfast.

Maggie showed me the airline page, that she'd typed up last night in the bar, and we had a go at adding a few, but we'd rather run out of steam. We thought of trying 'the way the animals would travel', but the only one we both liked was that a dog would sail in a barque. In the end we decided to leave things be, since it was all typed up and ready to go.

I said, 'I've done a lot of work on all this – do I get paid as a collaborator?'

'I think of you as an apprentice,' said Maggie. 'Which is an intellectual way of saying no, you don't. You've even had to buy me breakfast. Very good training for working for people like Nigel. You'll thank me one day.'

I didn't say anything. I was wondering whether to tell her there was a wasp climbing in to the jam, but I decided not to. She doesn't seem to like bad news about food.

Chapter Seven

We did the coast road to Clovelly, us and quite a few other drivers. It was pretty and flowery and wooded up there, and someone seemed to be throwing handfuls of seagulls up from below the cliffs from time to time.

Clovelly has car phobia. You have to leave the car in a park at the top of the cliff and teeter down the steep street on foot, tripping over cobblestones. Maggie was over the moon, although I think her red sandals would have complained if they knew how. 'Look,' she kept saying, 'it can be done, places don't have to be ruined by tourism.'

It is pretty, even I can see that. There are little white cottages with flowers in front, and some of them have things like huge wooden sledges lashed to their sides. When I asked Maggie about them, she said they weren't *like* wooden sledges, they *were* wooden sledges, and they were still sometimes used for dragging fish and provisions up and down the main street.

There were cats everywhere. Berwick would have been a problem here, he likes cats. He goes up to them to be friendly, but most cats misunderstand and get hysterical. These ones all looked very calm, strolling about and sitting on walls and washing their faces, but I suppose if you're cat-sized and fifty pounds of black mostly-labrador rushes you, you're wise to think the worst.

Then we staggered back up to the car and I was so tired that for once I was glad to get into it and sit down. I broke out the second tube of extra-strong mints and we wandered off towards somewhere called Great Torrington.

It began to get strange, I seem to remember, not long after Clovelly. The pretty stuff died away and we began to go through moor and marsh and big farms and then later on the road began to undulate and there were woods in among the farms.

'Haunted land around here,' said Maggie. So she felt it, too. 'Have you ever read *Tarka the Otter*?'

'I've heard of it.'

'It was set around here. A lot of it was set on the Torridge.'

'What's a Torridge?'

'It's a river. It goes out to sea at Appledore, with the River Taw.'

'We've seen its end,' I said. 'Now we're going to see its beginning. That's neat.'

'We won't get that far. We'll just see it passing by at Torrington.'

I said I thought it was a pity we weren't actually looking for the source of it. Maggie said it wouldn't be as dramatic as looking for the source of the Amazon.

'I didn't mean that,' I said. The car dipped down into a wooded valley and the first clouds of the day began to pass overhead. They were small ones, and quite far apart, so they sent shadows drifting across the landscape, like ghosts. Even though I was sitting down I was still tired and the road was going up and down, rocking the car like an old-fashioned cradle, and the passing cloud shadows were making my eyes feel sleepy. None of this had been real to me since we set out, but now it was getting even more dream-like. I found I was thinking out what to say for what seemed like a long time before I said it, instead of just rattling on as usual.

'I mean,' I said slowly, 'it's as if you're trying to find something, and if it was the source of a river it would be easy, because that's real, and we'd know if you'd done it or not.'

'That sounds very profound,' said Maggie.

'No,' I drifted off again, but not to sleep, my eyes were open. We drove off over a bridge, over the Torridge perhaps. It was very pretty. 'No, I mean you've got to look for Devon, haven't you? And write about it. That's your job for this week?'

'I suppose so, yes.'

'Well, it's too much, isn't it?' I said. I was blinking a lot because each time I got my eyes open they just wanted to close again. 'It's too big, and every bit of it's different. You'll never know if you've found it or not. But if it was a river source, you could stand there and say "That's it", and take a pic, and there we'd be.'

'It's not always that easy to find a river source,' said Maggie. She at least still sounded quite bright, was still answering quickly, as usual. 'Some of the Dartmoor ones start in a huge blanket bog. They gather themselves together from a vast area of wetness and gradually form a channel. In that case there's no one specific spot you can point to and say "That's it".'

I don't think she really understood what I meant. I'm not sure if I did, quite.

'Thing is,' I said, 'it's as though you're on a Quest, but nobody's going to know if you've found the thing you're Questing for.'

'Maybe you shouldn't take up journalism,' said Maggie. 'Maybe you should be a philosopher.'

'Or perhaps it's not a Quest,' I said. 'Perhaps it's a Task. That could explain it.'

'It's a task, all right.'

'No, I mean a Task with a capital T. Like the ones in fairy stories. Like the one where the princess had to sort out thousands of different kinds of seed and the ants helped her.'

'A Task is a more suitable idea for Devon,' said Maggie. 'Cornwall has all its stories of Arthur and the Knights of the Round Table, so Cornwall is a suitable place for a Quest. But Devon does go in for Tasks, rather. On Dartmoor there's something called Cranmere Pool. It isn't really a pool any more, it's just an area of marsh, part of the large blanket bog I was talking about. But in the days when it had water in it people used to think it was bottomless. It's said to be haunted by a character called Cranmere Benjie who was doomed, for his misdeeds, to empty it with a pierced seashell. If he ever succeeded – and you could say he did, since it isn't actually a pool any more – then he had to weave the sand at the bottom into ropes.'

'That makes me tired to think of it.'

'That isn't all. Okehampton Castle, on the edge of Dartmoor, is haunted by a Lady Howard, who was burnt as a witch. I think she murdered some husbands.'

'Whose husbands?'

'Oh, her own, I think. Anyway, her ghost is punished for her wickedness with a Task and a Half. She has to ride to the castle every night, from her home in Tavistock, in a carriage made of bone, driven by a headless coachman. It's a wonder they find the way, when you come to think of it. As far as I remember, the horses are headless, too, but the carriage dog that runs beside them has a head – with one eye in the centre of its forehead. It's a black dog, naturally. And her Task is to pluck all the grass from the castle mound, at the rate of a single blade a night.'

'But it would grow again before she could finish.'

'It does.'

I leant my head back against the seat and looked down the sides of my nose at the scenery through the front window. Looking at it like that, all I saw were different shapes, shapes of hills and valleys and trees and clouds.

'That makes what you have to do seem a bit easier,' I said.

'Easier, but similar,' said Maggie. 'I've got the nursery school version, those two were at university level.'

'That does explain it, though,' I said. 'It makes much more sense to me if it's not a Quest but a Task.'

'And knowing my luck,' said Maggie, 'I'll win a princess.'

'An Austin Princess, perhaps,' I said.

'You're sometimes a comfort to me,' said Maggie.

I'm not sure when I first realized we were beginning to get lost. It was after Great Torrington, where you park on a kind of inland cliff overlooking the river. That was where I picked up all the information leaflets I thought we hadn't already got, while Maggie clonked round the museum – from the Romans to the Victorians in two and a half minutes – and where we went round the Dartington Glass showroom. Maggie said there was as much Dartington stuff around Devon as there were pixies in Cornwall, and it was nice to see where it all came from. So if we hadn't found the start of the river, at least we'd found the source of the glass. We also found a bank that made a call to London and then passed Maggie a bit of cash.

It was also after we had lunch in a pub which didn't seem to mind me sitting inside it, and where I watched Maggie write down 'Friendly pub with real ale and good bar snacks.' She let me flick back through her notebook to see what she'd put down about all the other pubs she'd stopped the car to inspect, over the last few days. 'Doesn't vary much, does it?' I said. 'Don't you ever want to write "Hostile pub with filthy food and acrylic beer where the locals throw darts at the visitors"?'

'Oddly enough, no,' said Maggie.

It was after all that, it was when we began to go down small roads again, through woods and then through farmland where some of the farm buildings looked so old they seemed about to fall down.

It was quite late in the afternoon by this time. The little clouds in the sky had joined up into a sort of faint greyness overhead, which blocked out the sun and made some of the deep lanes, with their high hedges, very dim indeed. Also there was a vague kind of mistiness beginning to rise from the ground. It wasn't exactly that there was a fog – it was just that the sky seemed low and white and there were wafts of white misty stuff low on the ground and trapped in the lanes, and I couldn't help wondering what it would be like if the sky got lower, and the mist built up – and they met.

Then Maggie took to stopping the car at signposts and glaring at them, and then snatching up one of her maps and looking at it and muttering. The way Dad does, but the way Maggie generally doesn't.

There was something else that was different, too, and after a bit I realized what it was. We weren't seeing any other cars. There was only us.

There were good reasons for all of it. Maggie said the mist had come because there'd been rain in the night, then sun during the day, and also because we were between two big rivers, the Torridge and the Taw. Also, even Maggie must have been tired by then, and you can't hold place names and directions in your head when you're tired. And from what she'd said about the area, it was obvious there were unlikely to be convoys of cars at full throttle eager to get to it.

Still, it all made me uneasy. I kept thinking about Maggie saying there was nothing in mid-Devon, and I began to feel that this white vapoury stuff actually was The Nothing that she had heard of. Uneasiness and sleepiness and mist aren't a nice mixture.

Maggie re-found us when we crossed the A377, and we managed to take in Chumleigh and Chawleigh — I think they really are called that. But she wasn't bright and cheery any more, she was noticeably ratty, and she kept muttering about this being a total waste of time. I would have thought they were her sorts of places. Even I could see they were pretty, and with thatch, natch. Maggie said, 'They're fine, fine, but I've got to fit in Dartmoor and Dartmouth and Salcombe and Torbay and this just isn't working.' She was looking all flustered and cornered, the way she does when she comes to our house and she and Dad talk politics. Maggie's pink and he's blue. Between them they turn the air purple, Mum says. Mum's amber and clashes with both of them.

At the second place, whichever one that was, she homed in on a pub with a restaurant and said, 'We'd better eat dinner here. Things'll look better after food.'

I was amazed. It was only six-forty-five. In my opinion, it was a very good time to eat, hardly too late at all, but not Maggie's usual style. I asked if we were going to stay over here, and she said no, we had to get on. 'We'll work our way down through more of this mid-business,' she said, 'and stay overnight in Crediton. We can head off for the Moor from there in the morning.'

Dinner was unlike any of our other meals together. No sniping, no jokes. Maggie didn't even drink any wine. She just ate, sitting sideways to the table and folding and unfolding

90

various maps she'd brought in with us. The only thing she said to me was, 'Let him suggest I haven't tried and I will personally drag him down here and make him cover all the ground we've covered.' And she wasn't really saying that to me, anyway.

We ate home-made pies in little brown pots. I expect they were quite nice, but my tummy was churning around, perhaps I'd overdosed on mints, and I didn't enjoy mine much. Maggie ordered me an ice cream with fresh fruit sauce for afterwards. I didn't want it, but I think she felt guilty for snapping at me, so I ate some of it.

When we left, I said, 'Why can't we go straight to Crediton by the main road?'

I'd looked at the maps, too. I couldn't help it. Maggie had spread them out so far all over the table I couldn't have seen round them to look at anything else anyway.

'Because he wants us to look at mid-Devon and we're going to look at mid-Devon,' said Maggie savagely.

I think she thought she was punishing Nigel the Nurd by going on even when it was obviously useless. I've done things like that myself to get back at Mum or Dad, but it isn't encouraging to see an adult doing it, especially when it's the only known adult available.

We left and plunged off into the narrow lanes again, and it almost seemed to be dusk outside, it was so overcast. The mist was spooking around all over the fields and the high ground – and of course we got lost again.

I thought of saying, 'It can't be because you're drunk,' but I decided not to. I didn't feel it would be wise to say anything at all, the mood she was in.

I think one of the problems was that those roads wind around so much that it's possible to see a signpost pointing to a place on the left and then, not far on, to see a sign pointing to the same place, but on the right. Both roads probably go to the place in the end – but it does make you feel as though something or someone is getting at you.

'It's like driving round a bloody cat's cradle,' said Maggie, 'pardon my French.'

I did tell her the French don't say 'bloody' – but apart from that I kept quiet.

She'd stopped bothering with the map. 'If we just keep driving we're bound to hit a main road,' she said. 'Oh hell fire, look at these signposts.'

Narrow winding lanes, each one exactly like the last, wandered along to tiny crooked crossroads. When they got there, there was nothing, not a village, not even a house, just a signpost pointing to places like Poughill and Puddington – and even No-Man's Land.

'Nigel the Abominable No-Man,' said Maggie ferociously.

I grinned a bit at that, and she grinned a bit, and then she stopped the car, nowhere, for a moment, and said, 'Clare, I'm sorry, I'm being appalling. I've got a black dog on my shoulder and it certainly isn't Berwick.'

'A one-eye-in-the-middle-of-the-head job?'

'I think so,' she said. 'I'll be OK again in the morning. We'd better stop soon and have done with it. I'm tired and fed up and I've got a headache and a stiff neck.'

'Possibly withdrawal symptoms,' I said, 'from not having wine at dinner.'

Maggie flung the car into gear and started off again. 'If you're going to be spiteful,' she said, 'I'll stop apologizing.'

But just at that moment, as we curved around a bend in the misty-wisty lane, we saw one signpost, standing all on its own in a hedge, pointing off the road to the right, *Black Dog*, it said.

'I don't believe it,' said Maggie, and stopped the car right by it to look at it properly. 'Bad omen, or good?'

'Good!' I said. 'It's Berwick, guiding us.'

'Could be a headless wonder,' said Maggie, 'in the pay of the Devil.' But she obviously didn't think so, because she followed the sign.

It did help a lot. It wasn't that it led us anywhere special, because it didn't, it was just that it stopped Maggie battling up and down murky lanes in a rage. I suppose there must be a village called Black Dog, but we didn't see it. What we found was *The Black Dog* pub. Maggie parked outside it and took a map in to ask directions. Ordinarily I wouldn't have been wild about being left alone in the car in an empty lane with early dusk threatening, but because I thought Berwick had this bit in hand, or in paw, rather, I was quite relaxed about it.

Maggie came out and said Crediton was too far. They'd given her directions to a bed and breakfast place and had even phoned up to see if it could take us. For the first time ever, she shoved the map and the written directions at me, so I cracked the third tube of mints and half used the map and half used the directions, and we found it. Quite a big house, it was, with a front garden and a proper path and two other cars in the drive. It seemed like a teeming metropolis after where we'd been.

While a nice woman in a purple cardigan showed us to our rooms, Maggie asked if there was a telephone she could use. Why hadn't I thought of that? I'd been so caught up in the tangle of lanes and of Maggie's anxieties, which were far more frightening to me than my own, that I'd almost forgotten about home.

'There's no coin box,' said the woman, 'but you're welcome to use our phone.'

'That's very kind,' said Maggie. 'I'll reverse the charges.'

As soon as we got our stuff in to our rooms, Maggie said to me, 'Get to bed as soon as you can. Even I'm going to. Tomorrow will be a better day, I promise.'

'OK,' I said.

I heard her go downstairs and I sorted out a few off my bits and pieces. Then I took my washing bag and went out on to the landing to cross over to the bathroom on the other side. And that's all I was doing when I heard what Maggie said on the phone, I wasn't eavesdropping, I really wasn't.

The first thing I heard her say, as I closed my bedroom door quietly behind me, was, 'Thank God I've caught you in at last, I could hardly reverse the charges to the hospital.' I walked across the landing to the bathroom door quite

94

normally, I didn't creep, but trainers don't make any noise. I realized Maggie didn't know I was just up above her when I heard what she said next. She said, 'Look, if something awful's going to happen, you *must* tell me straight out, I must get this child back, it's only fair.'

Then I did stand still and listen. I couldn't have moved if I'd wanted to, I felt as if all at once I was made of nothing but bones, with nothing to move them. There was a long silence and then Maggie said, 'When?'

After that, I could move. I don't know why that did it. I went in to the bathroom and stood by the basin and ran the water and splashed my fingers under it for quite a long time. I didn't wash, that seemed too complicated.

When I came out, Maggie wasn't on the phone any more. I went to her bedroom door and knocked on it.

'Come in,' said Maggie.

'Did you get through?' I said in a very normal voice.

'Yes,' said Maggie. 'I got your father. I was going to look in and say goodnight and tell you. Everybody's OK and we're ringing again tomorrow.'

So whatever was going on, I was still to be kept out of it.

'Oh good,' I said. 'Goodnight, Maggie.'

'Are you all right?' said Maggie.

I said, 'I'm really tired. I just want to go to bed.'

'Of course,' said Maggie. 'We won't get up until eight tomorrow.'

I closed her door and went back to my room,

my little slanty-ceiling'd room where Berwick, I thought then, had arranged for me to be so that I'd find out what I needed to know, and could do something about it.

Chapter Eight

I wondered how I'd managed to be so stupid up to
then. I'd known perfectly well, all the time, that
things were very wrong and looking back it was
quite obvious to me that Maggie had known, too.
But because this trip was so different from normal life I had somehow forgotten that normal life
was still going on at home, and that if something
was wrong it was quite likely to get wronger.

At that moment, it was all perfectly clear to
me. They hadn't sent me off just because Mum
was in hospital and Dad was practically living at
the office and they didn't want me to be alone.
They'd sent me off with Maggie into her unreal
world to try to protect me from something nasty
that was going on in the real world. But you can't
do that, you see, because if something nasty did
happen, to Mum or to the baby, I would be
knocked out by it wherever they'd sent me, even
if they'd stuck me up on a space station among
the stars.

And if Maggie had to tell me some horrible
thing while we were living like this, it wouldn't
make any sense to me. It would get all mixed up
with ghosts and goats and Lynmouth floods, and
I wouldn't really believe it – so I wouldn't know
how to think about it or what to do.

If I was at home, it would different. I'd be sleeping in my own room under my own posters. I'd be helping Dad do his fry-up, which is all he can cook, and working out how to get at the chips he always knocks down the back of the cooker without actually making him move it. I'd be having the conversation about whether Berwick should have a new food bowl or whether he actually likes his old one, with the chew marks around the rim. Then I'd be able to understand properly what was going on. I might not like it, but I'd know what I thought about it.

I didn't want to ask Maggie to take me home. I was sure she'd try and talk me out of it, and anyway it didn't seem quite fair. She had her Great Task to do, and I didn't want to be one of the obstacles she had to overcome. Looking at the map in the restaurant, and the car, I'd noticed that there was a railway line which ran past us over to the west and then curved down south of us to Crediton station. Crediton was too far, but there were smaller stations along the route. One in particular, I could picture in my mind, was more or less directly west of us. Despite buying breakfast, I still had most of the cash Dad had given me when he saw us off. I would go home by train. I would take my blue shoulder bag with me, and I would leave my main luggage and a note for Maggie.

It's hard to explain what a sensible, practical idea this seemed when I worked it out in the little slanty ceiling'd bedroom.

I turned all my belongings out of both bags and inspected them. When you're going home it doesn't much matter what you take, because there'll always be spares when you get there, so all I had to worry about was the journey. I didn't want to weigh myself down because I knew it must be quite a long walk to the station. I took my money. I took my washing things. I don't know if I was expecting to wash on the train, or what, but it seemed to me that sensible people pack washing things and it comforted me to think I was being sensible. I took my funny little compass. It was only a cheap one, but if I turned it around, the needle always pointed the same way, so I supposed it worked. I took an extra jumper and the last clean pair of socks. I was very impressed at how sensible I was being. It almost made me feel I wasn't going alone but had some other sensible person with me. Also, I took all the half-eaten packs of mints I could round up from various pockets. Unfortunately, I couldn't take a map. They were locked in the car, or perhaps with Maggie in her room. Either way I couldn't get one without asking her, but I had a photograph in my head of the one we'd looked at most recently, in the car.

I left a note, right in the middle of the bed where Maggie couldn't miss it, and I weighted it down with a shoe on either side so it wouldn't blow away in the draught when she opened the door. I calculated that she'd only have a few minutes' worry. She'd find it when she came to wake me in the morning, and by then I'd be safely at home. She would telephone our house at once, as the note told her to, and I would answer, and she'd be able to start her day with a clear mind. As Dad says.

The only thing I wished was that she'd got hold

of Dad earlier so that I could have known earlier what I had to do. It was nearly nine o'clock and it was seriously dimpsey outside and I knew that in the country they don't fight back when the night comes, by putting on lights and all that, they just more or less let it happen. Still, the station was bound to have lights, and the railway line, I was sure, followed the main road, so there'd be the noise and lights of the traffic on that. If, as seemed likely, I didn't get right to the station before dark, all these various lights would guide me. Also, when you're heading for an obvious place like a railway station, anybody can direct you.

That was what I thought.

I got down the stairs quietly and I got to the front door and I turned the button on the Yale lock and I pulled the door towards me. It didn't move. It had a big round brown handle halfway down, as well as the Yale at eye level, so I put my bag on the floor – I could imagine it swinging forward the way shoulder bags do and clonking against the door – and took the Yale knob in one hand the brown handle in the other, and turned them both at once, and pulled. Nothing happened. I tried again, this time turning the brown handle the other way. That didn't work, either.

They'd obviously double-locked the door in some way. I couldn't bear it. My mind was already striding out for the station, and I couldn't possibly bring it back and make it stay here the night. My body simply had to catch up with it. I thought of telling the purple woman I wanted to go for a walk before I went to bed, but that was obviously no good, she'd be bound to tell Maggie.

I thought of trying to climb out of a window, but I haven't had much practice at that sort of thing, and I was sure I'd make a noise and be caught.

I looked at the door again and saw that it couldn't be double-locked because there wasn't another keyhole, just the Yale and the handle. Then I saw it. Close under the round brown handle, so you could only see it if you crouched down a little, was a small silvery bolt. I pulled it and it slid back easily and I thought – that was a test. Something was testing me to see if I was really determined to go.

With the bolt back, the door opened easily, and I sidled out. I closed it as quietly as I could, but of course the Yale lock clunked as it slipped into place. I stood where I was in the porch, quite still, so that if anyone had raised a head and listened after that clunk, at least they wouldn't hear anything else straightaway, which might make them think they'd been mistaken. Nothing seemed to happen inside the house. I decided to risk making a quick trip to the gate and through it. I avoided the gravel path, reached out and opened the gate, did a peculiar lop-sided jump through it so as not to make a final scrunch on the gravel, and was behind the hedge in the lane outside.

I would rather have kept still after each separate movement, so that the people in the house would have forgotten one sound before they heard the next, and wouldn't get suspicious, but the light was going and the mist wasn't and I didn't want to hang around.

I got to the end of the short lane and turned into the narrow road which I was sure led in the

101

general direction of the station. I was feeling very pleased with myself because I'd passed the first test – the bolt. Then I stopped feeling pleased because I realized that if that really had been a test, then there might be more, and I didn't like the idea of failing, out here by myself, alone with Devon.

The air was the colour of dirty paintwater, and although I could still see everything, nothing looked quite right. The hedges on either side looked unreal, and the one or two trees growing in the hedges looked unreal, and I didn't like the way the narrow road ahead curved out of sight. Mostly, when you go round a corner there's just more of the same, but you can't ever be sure. I wouldn't have been all that surprised – I don't think – to have come on a room from Watermouth Castle with life-sized gruesome figures crouching in it, and then springing out at me as I walked towards them and broke an infra-red beam. I know how it's done, you see, but it still gives me a fright.

I thought I'd be glad when I got round the bend and Watermouth Castle wasn't there, so I walked faster, but it wasn't the sort of bend you ever do get round, it just went on bending, ever so slightly. I began to think the road must go round in a circle, but at last it began to bend, ever so slightly, in the other direction. According to the compass I wasn't going west as I should, just a bit north and then a bit south, and so on, but at least I was never going east, so I supposed it all evened out at west in the end.

Then I began to feel it wasn't just the hedges and trees and murky light that were unreal. It

102

was also the corners-that-weren't-really-there, and the fact that the road had no proper direction, and everything, all of it.

All that was real was me, with my blue bag, walking down the middle of the road listening out for cars, and Mum and Dad and everyone at home.

Maggie wasn't real. She had been, a bit, but now she was swallowed up in that house that you'd probably never find again if you came back some other year and looked for it, and the house itself was swallowed up by the unreal bend in the road behind me.

I've never felt so out of place in my life, and I knew that Devon felt I was out of place, too. I thought, at that point, that it didn't like me because I was real and it wasn't. Now I know that I was wrong about the reason – but right about it not liking me.

The road meandered on and the moon rose above the horizon. The sky was so dark now that I couldn't see the cloud overhead, but I knew it was still there because it made the moon look so weird. It looked like a fuzzy patch of whiteness, with no edges. This patch of round fuzzy light was so big that I realized the moon must be full. It didn't seem to be giving out any light. It seemed that the cloud was sopping up all the light, which was just spreading across it like a stain and not going anywhere else. Yet it must have been giving out something because I could see where I was going, just about, and there was nowhere else any light could have been coming from. There were no stars. I was glad of that because although the moon is sort of real, stars aren't. Light takes years and years to reach us from them so the ones you think you see may not even be there any more. Well, they probably are, because they'd have done a programme on TV if any stars had exploded or anything. But they quite likely aren't where they seem to be any more. The light we see comes from their past.

To the left the ground sloped upwards a bit and to the front there was a big bank of extra-black cloud coming up. I saw that there was a milky white ground mist coming out of the earth to the left, like steam. In fact, it was hovering just above the ground, not on it. I could see that if I walked through it my feet would be visible, and so would my head and shoulders, but the rest of me would be lost. It looked as though this was the place where they grew the mist, this was the source of it all, and all the wisps and patches that had been building up in the last few hours had come from here.

The black seemed to be closing in ahead, and the sickly white was getting deeper on the left, and I was just wondering which of them looked the more horrid when, with no warning or sign of anything, the road forked. My compass, which I could just see to read, offered me a choice of south-west or north-east. I took south-west, and that was when I realized that the blackness wasn't low cloud at all, it was trees, a wood.

This, I thought, is where I step over into some awful world which is even more unreal than before. I felt a bit sick. I worked a mint out of the packet in my pocket without stopping to take the packet out, and I put it in my mouth.

I could hear water. There was a little stream

somewhere and for a stupid moment I almost thought of finding it and following it. Then I realized that it might not be going anywhere I'd want to be. I might even follow it in the wrong direction and end up sucked down into Maggie's blanket bog. The poor old ghost with the pierced seashell wouldn't be able to weave a rope of sand in time to pull me out, I could bet on that.

When I had set out with the compass, it hadn't occurred to me that even if I could see to read it, which was getting increasingly difficult, the roads wouldn't let me walk in exactly the direction I chose. Even now that I saw the problem there was nothing I could do about it. One thing I knew for sure was that I was not going to cut across country.

I still had a kind of conviction that if I kept going mainly west I was bound to strike the road and the railway line. Even if I was off course for the station, I reasoned, I could follow the track until I got there. But I was also beginning to think that if the roads around here could even shake Maggie off course, I probably didn't stand a very good chance.

I shifted the blue bag to my other shoulder. It was quiet, but there were sounds. Just as I couldn't see in detail, so I couldn't hear in detail, either. I was just aware of faint sighings and rustles from the wood. I couldn't tell if there was something moving in there, or if what I was hearing was just it being alive, just it being a wood.

Trees definitely have two personalities, a day-time one and a night-time one. In the day-time they're all about leaves and fruit and shade, and

105

branches for climbing, and holes for birds to nest in. Cosy. At night they're about something else entirely, and it isn't anything that a human being could ever understand. It isn't cosy at all.

I knew I would feel a lot happier when I got past that wood.

There was a very faint sound that sometimes came from behind me as I walked, a sort of scrat-scrat. As though perhaps something was following me. Something that didn't draw its claws in when it walked. It wasn't a Berwick-dog. It was something quite small, and strangely enough that made it more unsettling.

I looked round but I couldn't see anything. I thought maybe it wasn't on the road at all, maybe it was off to the side somewhere.

I was sure I mustn't run. If I began to run I might not be able to stop. It was fine for Berwick to guide me here, I thought, but it would be an awful lot nicer if he was here too. If something scrat-scratted at Berwick, he would take decisive action.

I started to try to think sensible thoughts about what I was doing, and about how it would be when I got on to the train. Then, of course, I began to wonder if there would be a train as late as this. Even if there was, it might not go straight to London. I might have to change. By which time it would be even later, and perhaps the last train from the second place would have gone. I'd have to spend the night on the station. Stations are creepy when they're empty.

Scrat-scrat from behind. A quick look over my shoulder, but no sign of movement. As I turned back I smelt my own pepperminty breath. It was quite reassuring.

If stations are creepy, woods are worse. Was the scrat-scrat thing a second test? That reminded me of the bolt. And thinking of that reminded me that now the door would be unbolted all night. Should I ring the purple woman from the station and tell her? I couldn't, I hadn't got her number or name.

Dad says worries always hunt in packs, and he's right. What made it worse, though, was that these weren't just worries, they were facts. Fact: Mum and the baby were in trouble. Fact: I might be lost. Fact: I was probably being followed. Fact: I had very likely missed the last train. Fact: I might have exposed Maggie and the others to some horrible danger by leaving the door unbolted. Fact: Devon didn't like me. Fact: coming out here on my own at night was the stupidest thing I'd ever done and I wouldn't be at all surprised if the next anyone heard of me was in some gruesome shock-horror item on the TV news.

Scrat-scrat. Nothing there. Was it a small sound close to or a larger sound farther off?

Scrat. I stopped and put the bag down on the road. I stood still and I looked and looked all around, turning very slowly. I thought I could hear my heart beating. The moon was higher, but still fuzzy and spilt-looking. I could see a short stretch of road between two curves. I could see dark woods on one side, whose trees seemed to be thinning out. I could see where they seemed to come to an end. I could see a hedge and higher ground on the other side. The ground mist was still there, but the sky mist was turning into tiny drops of water.

There was just a little bit of wind. It hadn't been there before. It was annoying the trees of the wood a bit, making them shift about in their sleep. No, that was wrong, they weren't asleep, they were wide awake. That was what was so disturbing about them.

The scrat didn't move. It was waiting for me.

It wasn't that I believed I could do anything to put things right for Mum once I was home, it was that I believed, or sort of believed, that I was working a kind of magic by trying to get there. Some people think they have to get clear of the bathroom before the lavatory stops flushing, some people think they have to get home without treading on the cracks in the pavement. I just had to get myself back from Devon – and my reward would be that Mum and the baby would be OK.

It wasn't going to be easy, though. Devon could re-arrange its roads and move its woods about and drive me in any direction it liked, because it wasn't real, so it didn't have to stick to any rules. It had already begun messing about in the afternoon, when even Maggie began to realize that the roads as they lay on the ground weren't very much like the roads that were drawn on the map.

I put the blue bag over my shoulder. As I did, the scrat sounded right in my ear. It was as though the thing had jumped on my shoulder.

I dragged the bag off again, and turned my head, and as I did I could see that it was the long tag of the shoulder strap that had been scratting on the back of my anorak as I moved. It only did it when the bag was on my right shoulder, not when it was on my left.

I don't know why, but it was at that moment, when I was all full of relief, that I understood why Devon didn't like me, why the trees were grumbling and the roads were sulking and the mist was mauling at me, and all that.

It wasn't because I was real and it wasn't. It was because it was all just as real as me, but I was refusing to admit it, had refused to admit it ever since I got there.

I suppose all holiday places seem a bit unreal, and if you skitter across them at high speed, like a water-boatman skittering across the surface of a pond, they seem even less real than they otherwise might. I don't suppose, though, that any of them like being treated like that.

'All right, place,' I said, walking down the dark road which was beginning to slope quite steeply away from me. 'I'm sorry.' I said it quite quietly, in a whisper really, because I didn't expect it to understand my words, just my meaning. 'You are real, you've always been real. I got it wrong. Now will you please put the roads back where they were and let me get to the station?'

Ahead I thought I could see the shape of a small house, but it had no lights. I knew that nothing in this world would make me knock at its door to ask directions, I had no choice but to go on walking towards it because it was right on the road, but I walked on the opposite side, and I went quite slowly so that when I was nearly at it, I would be able to run right past. I can't explain why. I knew it was probably just dark because the people were out for the evening, or away.

People in Devon very likely go on holiday just like the rest of us. It seemed to me, though, that it was dark because it was lying in wait for me.

I said, 'I'm sorry Devon. Of course you're real. I'm not just saying it, I believe it now.'

The thing I hate about talking to yourself is that you don't get answers so you don't know how you're doing. Not that I was talking to myself, not really.

The house was nearly level with me, squarish and black, thick black, the kind of black that could suck you in and swallow you. I didn't take to my heels – I've never been able to work out how people do that. I took to my toes, and I ran until I was well past it, until my breath hurt. I had been right not to run from the scrat. Once I started it was very difficult to stop.

When I did stop I had to put the bag on the ground and find a tissue. I needed to blow my nose. It seemed I was crying.

Where were all the people I'd thought I would ask for directions? Why had I ever thought there would be any?

I came to a crooked T-Junction. The compass said it went north or south. I took south. It somehow seemed nearer to west that north did, I can't say why. It didn't seem to have stopped tying me up in its roads.

Even now that I knew what the scrat-scrat had been, I didn't feel much happier about it. I kept thinking perhaps the place had used the strap tag to tap me on the shoulder – Scrat-scrat, pay attention to me, I'm more important and powerful than you and your kind will ever be.

Dark and sloping this lane was, and there was

an awful smell of earth, as though things were heaving their roots around in the ground and disturbing it. I suppose it was the misty rain causing that. People are quite wrong when they say that if you understand the cause of things they're not frightening any more.

I looked behind me up the slope of the dark road and from the other side of the rise there came a faint sort of glow that seemed to be growing. If there was one thing I really didn't need it was another test.

Then I heard the sound that went with the glow. It was a car. I knew I wasn't going to stop it, but what if it stopped me? I thought it was quite likely that it would. I began to walk backwards, so that I'd know when it came over the rise. I could tell that it was travelling very slowly. That seemed as menacing as the house being dark. It was as though it was creeping up on me. Because why would it go slowly – travelling in the dark, in the country, it must be able to see that there were no lights, no other traffic, it must know it could go much faster. Then I realized, of course, it was going to the little black house – it was the people from there, back from their evening out, driving slowly so as to turn in at their drive. With the car and the house both made harmless in the same moment, I turned my back on them and marched on down the road. As Maggie had said, keep going and you're bound to get somewhere.

Splat, my shadow fell on the ground in front of me, and at the same moment a wormy, furry thing with four legs and a mean little head bounded across the road and leapt into the hedge. I don't know which of us was more frightened – the animal who had been hit by my black shadow, or me. The car had not stopped at the house, it had crept on over the rise and caught me in its headlights, I leapt for the hedge almost as quickly as the animal had, and burst right through it and crouched in the dark and earth-smelling field on the other side.

The car didn't speed up or slow down or hoot. It just rolled on, very very slowly, with the engine purring very quietly, sending its yellow light down the road ahead. Little fingers of the light crept through the hedge to me, but I knew that even if they touched me, the car couldn't see me.

In the little bits of growing light I could see that the hedge was made up of separate bushes, growing very closely together, which was why I had managed to push through between two of them. Even so, I'm sure I couldn't have done it if I hadn't been so frightened. As I crouched there I became aware that my right foot was wet, where I had splashed into the ditch, and that the backs of my hands were scratched.

The car stopped. The engine cut out. I was tempted to run, across the field, anywhere, but I felt that was what it meant me to do. It must have seen me. It must be wondering where I'd gone. It was going to stay still and flush me out. If I kept very still myself, it would probably decide it had been mistaken and go on.

I knew that it standing still like this might not even be sinister. It might be that it thought I was a sheep or something, loose in the road, that ought to be rounded up. No, it must have seen me better than that. Well, perhaps it would decide it had been mistaken. Perhaps it would decide it had seen Cranmere Benjie, taking a break from his sand-plaiting, or Lady Howard, stretching her legs before picking the next blade of grass.

The car lights went out.

That was horrible. Especially as the dark was darker after the light.

Then a faint, dim light seemed to come on, behind the hedge. It was going to come after me with a torch.

I very nearly panicked and took off across the fields then, but what stopped me was that I hadn't heard the door open or anyone get out. It was just the other side of the hedge – no one could get out of a car so quietly that I wouldn't hear something, not even if they didn't shut the door. It was a trick to make me move. I stayed exactly where I was. It was another test. Please, Devon, I said in my head, I think you're asking too much of me.

Nothing happened. I imagined the wormy furry thing and me, both hiding, both listening, both waiting. And the car waiting, too, waiting and glowing.

And still nothing happened.

There comes a time when nothing happening seems more frightening than something horrible happening. I had to know what it was. I wasn't about to stand up and look over the hedge in case I found that something on the other side was looking back at me, but I could see that above my head and to the left a little was a biggish hole with broken twigs around it. I think it must have been where I had burst through. Moving very, very slowly, and keeping myself behind the thickest part of the hedge, I raised my head, very carefully, so I could just see out of the hole with one eye. If anything was looking that way, I knew it would probably see the white of my face, but I couldn't help it, I had to know. It didn't occur to me till much later that I could have rubbed mud on my face.

Not that it would have been necessary. Nothing was looking at me. The car was standing still in the road, just about six feet back from where I'd gone in to the hedge. Its headlights and sidelights were out, but the inside light was on. Sitting inside, quite still, looking straight ahead, was Maggie.

But just as I was about to stand up and call out to her in relief, I saw the state she was in. Maggie was crying. There were black lines of mascara running down her face, and even from that distance, and even though the wipers were going, I could see that her nose was quite red. She was just sitting there, in the car, staring straight ahead, crying.

I knew at once what had happened. Dad had rung back, the awful, unthinkable thing had happened. Maggie had gone to my room to break the news to me, and had found the note, and had come looking.

It was superstition, I know now, but I thought that if I didn't go to her and hear it, it still might not be true. If I refused to take the news, stayed in hiding, somehow managed to make it back home tonight, then everything would be all right after all. It may not have been a very sensible idea, but sensible ideas don't work when you're alone in the dark.

114

I stayed where I was.

Time seemed to go on and on, while Maggie sat there in her car and I stayed in the hedge, convinced that I was working my own magic. She can't have been sure of what she'd seen or she'd have come calling for me. Perhaps, what with the crying and the wipers, she hadn't seen clearly at all. She was just waiting on the off chance, with the light on so I could see her. She'd move on soon. She was bound to.

She did. Quite suddenly the glow went out, then the brighter lights came on and the engine started up again. I'd done it, I'd passed the next test.

Chapter Nine

I waited for the sound of the car to fade away
completely. It seemed to take ages because Maggie was driving so slowly, and when it got very
faint, so that it didn't seem any more important
than the faint movement of the wind in the trees,
I found I didn't really know if I could still hear it
or not.

I decided I couldn't, and I climbed back
through the hedge. I was careful not to step in
the ditch again. The scratches on my hands, and
the wetness of my foot, and the fact that I was
faintly damp all over, were all the more noticeable when I was back on the road.

The mist from the ground had met the low
cloud in the sky, just as I'd been afraid it would.
It was very uncomfortable because what happened when they did meet was that the air
became full of little tiny drops of wetness. I was
being mugged by a cloud.

I felt much lonelier since I'd seen Maggie.
When she drove away she somehow took with
her my idea that I was being guided by Berwick.
Poor old Berwick – he was probably asleep at
that moment, in a heap on his favourite tweed
skirt, in the corner of some dog cell. How could I
have thought he was arranging anything? He

116

probably didn't even know where he was, let alone where I was.

I began to walk at once, as fast as I could, in the direction I had been going, the direction Maggie had gone. I could tell that if I hung around I might not be able to move at all. Something peculiar had happened when I'd admitted to Devon that it was real; something peculiar and very unfair. It had become more threatening instead of less.

You see, the point was this – when I was real and it wasn't, however much it rustled its branches at me and blew on me with its wet-earth breath, I could shrug it off like you shrug off a horror movie. But now that it was real, too, there was no knowing what might happen that I wouldn't be able to shrug off. Also, it was bigger than me.

I'd got out beyond the wood, which was a bit better because you can never tell what might be in a wood, apart from the trees, and the trees were bad enough on their own. There were still the hedges along the sides of the road, though, and you can't tell what's behind hedges, either.

Then something different started to happen. A faint light appeared in the sky, over to the left, moved slowly across to the right and then disappeared. That is, I thought it was in the sky, but just before it disappeared I realized that the road sloped downwards in front of me towards a bit of a dip, and then the land sloped up again on the other side, and the light was actually on the ground, way up ahead. It wasn't a clear light, it was just a vague yellowness, like the moon was a vague whiteness. At first I thought it might be the

Devon pixies, out with their lanterns, trying to lead me somewhere awful.

The road met a crooked crossroad again, and the compass said that this time I could go directly west, so I did. I thought the station or at least the railway line, must be getting nearer by now. I didn't let myself look at my watch. I didn't want to know how late it was.

The faint glow appeared again, far far ahead, and moved across the countryside very slowly, and then seemed to go out.

It was Maggie, of course. Maggie was cruising around these horrible lanes, crying, looking for me to tell me – well, to give me some news. And I was plodding along them, crying, avoiding her. It was silly, I could see that. Silly to have gone off alone, silly to have hidden from Maggie, silly to invent all these tests for myself, silly to think there was some sort of magic that would make everything all right if I could just get home without hearing the truth.

I seemed to be stuck with it, though. There were only two things I could do, keep on walking like this, or else sit down in the wet road, which didn't sound like a lot of fun.

So I walked, pad pad pad, and I shifted the blue bag regularly from one shoulder to the other, and half the time it went scrat scrat scrat and half the time it didn't, and the glow of Maggie's lights, sometimes dim and sometimes almost bright, came and went all around me, maybe a mile this way, maybe a mile that way, but never down my dark road.

The road got down to the bottom of its dip and I could hear that there was a little stream somewhere off to the left. I couldn't tell if it was another little stream or the one I'd passed some time back. It was talking to itself, the way streams do, and it might have been nice company if all streams around here didn't make me think they were probably bringing news from the Dartmoor blanket bog, and perhaps some grains of sand that had slipped through Cranmere Benjie's boney fingers. I kept walking, in the middle of the road, and didn't go near.

The road began on one of its creepy bends, but then almost immediately there was another crossroads. I don't know why I call them crossroads. None of them were the shape of a cross, no two roads were opposite each other. This, like the others, was just a place where you had a choice of four directions. There was a signpost in the hedge, but I didn't try to read it. Without a map, nothing it said would mean anything to me anyway. I didn't look at the compass either. I just squatted down on my heels – I was really tired by then – and ate my last extra-strong mint, and waited. They say that if you wait long enough at Piccadilly Circus everyone you know will come by. I don't know if that's true, but I did think that as the only two people who seemed to be on the move tonight were Maggie and me, if one of us waited at a junction, then the other was quite likely to pass by eventually.

She took a long time about it. She kept glowing and fading all over the place, without ever getting really close. Sometimes I actually heard the engine, and stood up, but then the sound and the glow would drift off somewhere else – and of course she was doing it all so slowly. It was much

worse than waiting for a bus. I forgot about being
scared, and worried, and wet, and all of those
things, and began to get ratty instead. Oh come
on, I thought, how many roads can there *be*
around here?

She came at last, drifting down from the right,
and I went and stood in the middle of the lane. She
stopped. She was riding with the inside light on all
the time now, so I didn't have any nasty moments,
wondering if it really was her. I opened the door
and got in and sat down next to her. Then, because
she looked so awful, I remembered how scared I
was about Mum. She didn't start the car again at
once, she sort of stared at me and blew her nose a
lot, and then she said, 'Are you all right?'

'Wet, that's all,' I said.

'There aren't any more trains tonight,' she said.

'I was afraid of that,' I said.

'It's only a branch line, anyway,' she said.

'I was afraid of that, as well,' I said.

Then we just went on looking at each other. 'It's
all right,' I said, 'go on, you can tell me. Get it over
with.'

'I'm not going to tell you off,' said Maggie, who
didn't seem to have heard properly. 'I wish you
hadn't disappeared, but I think I understand why
you did.'

'Tell me about Mum,' I said. I didn't want to
hang around, now, I wanted to get on with it.

'Lovey,' said Maggie, 'you know the news. I told
you what your father said this evening. They're
all just waiting for the big event.'

'I thought Dad must have rung back – to say
something bad had happened.'

Maggie shook her head.

120

'Why did you come after me, then?'

'Why? Why do you think? I thought you seemed a bit unsettled so I went to your room to say goodnight, and I found the note. Once I'd seen that, *obviously* I came after you.' Her voice was getting a bit stronger. 'Thank God I looked in tonight,' she said, 'I might not have found it till tomorrow morning.'

'Well, but if there's nothing wrong at home, Maggie, why are you crying?' I said. 'It is all right to mention it, isn't it? Only it is rather obvious.'

'You are *so* dim,' said Maggie. 'I didn't know where you might be, I didn't know what might have happened to you, I didn't know what to do, I didn't know if I'd ever be able to find you, I had visions of having to tell them I'd lost you, I don't think I've ever been so frightened in my life. Clare, I'm not used to this kind of responsibility, and you don't half load it on.'

So Maggie had been crying about me. 'I didn't know you cared,' I said, and it came out a bit off-hand, but only because I was embarrassed.

Maggie didn't seem to mind. She put out her one arm and gave me a quick hug, and then started the car up and went on at a bit of a better pace. 'You smell awful,' she said.

The heater was on and the mud from the ditch and the damp from the cloud were steaming off me.

'It's Devonbreath,' I said. 'I smell like Berwick.'

'On a dog, it works,' said Maggie.

When we got back to the house ('Don't worry, I know *all* the roads now,' Maggie said) all the lights seemed to be on and the hall seemed to be full of people walking about and banging into each other. There were the purple woman and her beige husband and another two or three visitors, the ones with the other cars, I suppose. I realized that while I'd been getting nowhere out there, they'd all been making plans, synchronizing watches, and preparing to call the police and to get out there themselves if Maggie wasn't back with me by whenever. If I hadn't been so tired, I'd have been *really* embarrassed then.

Maggie was great. She gave them hundred watt smiles all round, which made them feel good, and got rid of them, and ran me a hot bath, and the purple woman's husband put my clothes in the airing cupboard and said the mud would come off when they were dry, and the purple woman made me cocoa, and then Maggie came in and sat on my bed while I drank it, and it was just us again.

'Cocoa all right?' she said.

'Nice,' I said. 'Except for the skin.'

'Stir it.'

'I have. The skin broke up and bits of it keep crouching on my top lip.'

'Look,' said Maggie, 'people make decisions for all the right reasons, but that doesn't necessarily mean they're the right decisions.'

'I know that now,' I said. 'But it really did seem like a good idea at the time.'

'I'm sure. I don't mean you. I mean your parents. Things are a bit dicey with the baby, and you were right to think they wanted you out of the way – but it's only because they love you and they were trying to make things easier for you. Normally I wouldn't interfere, but if I don't tell you properly you're just going to run away from me again.'

'I didn't run away – I was just going home. Trying to, anyway.'

'Do you know what a Caesarian is?'

'When they unzip you and take the baby out that way?'

'Right. Well that's how this baby's going to be born. They're getting your mother rested, waiting for the right moment.'

The cocoa was drying on my top lip. I began to pick it off, carefully. 'She managed to have me,' I said. 'Why is it harder the second time? Shouldn't it be easier?'

'Well . . . ' said Maggie doubtfully.

'Oh no!' I said.

'What?' said Maggie.

I said, 'This is where you tell me I was adopted, and I crack up all over again. How old do you have to be to have a nervous breakdown?'

'I'm first in the queue for one of those,' said Maggie. 'You'll have to wait your turn. No, Clare, you weren't adopted, but you were born by Caesarian, too. I thought she might have told you by now.'

'No,' I said.

'Haven't you ever wondered about the scar?'

I thought about that. 'I've never seen her undressed,' I said. 'Even on the beach she wears a one-piece.'

'Yes, of course. Well there's a reason for all of that. She didn't want you to know until she felt you were old enough to cope with it. But you see the problem is that if you leave a thing like that, it's hard to decide when the day comes that someone *is* old enough. She just didn't want you to be worried.'

I said I thought I got more worried when I was being saved from worries than when I was allowed to have a really good go at them.

Maggie said she could understand that. 'I'm developing a philosophy,' she said, 'that says that healthy worry is actually good for you. Far better than excessive physical exercise. It keeps the weight down, stimulates the heart, cures constipation . . .'

'When does this thing happen?' I said.

'Day after tomorrow.'

I thought about it for a bit. Maggie watched me.

'But Maggie,' I said, 'a Caesarian isn't really such a big deal, is it? I've heard of people who've had them.'

'It rather depends on why it's necessary,' said Maggie. 'Look, this is "straight truth" time, OK? After you were born, your mother was told she must never have another baby.'

I said, 'It was that bad?'

Maggie looked at me quite steadily. 'We nearly lost you both,' she said.

'So why . . . ?'

'It was an accident, completely unexpected. They were all for terminating the pregnancy, right at the beginning, but she wouldn't allow that. She said it was meant, and she knew it would be all right. So now the hospital has to prove her right.'

'Maggie? Is she going to die?' I felt better when I'd used the word.

Maggie was still looking me straight in the eye – they say you shouldn't trust people who do that, but you can with Maggie, I've found.

124

'No,' said Maggie. 'There's always an element of risk in any operation, but this time it's extremely slight. They've got her in there – they have, they tell us, got her "stablized". They know, this time, what the problems are and they're ready for them. Unless something completely unexpected happens – and I mean *completely* unexpected – your mother is going to be all right.'

'And the baby?'

Maggie looked away from me. 'Your mother says the baby's going to be fine,' she said. 'All we can do is believe she's right.'

I picked off the last bit of dried cocoa. It had got nearly all the way up to my nose, I'm always a sloppy drinker when I'm upset.

'We'll make an early start in the morning,' said Maggie, 'and go straight back. OK?'

I thought about it. 'But Mum doesn't want me there,' I said.

'*Only* for your sake,' said Maggie. 'For her own sake, of course she wants to see you.'

'Will it give her a shock if we suddenly appear? Will she think it means something's gone wrong?'

'Not if we explain.'

'But if we suddenly turn up when we're not supposed to,' I said, 'she might think we've been told things are really bad. Maybe it's that it'll be all right as long as she *believes* it'll be all right.'

'I think that is the way she sees it,' said Maggie.

'Well then we could give her a fright and make it all go wrong. I think we ought to do it like we've been programmed to do it.'

125

'We were programmed to stay away until the op's over, and then whizz straight back,' said Maggie.

'We'll do that, then,' I said. I was sure all the dried cocoa had been accounted for, but I gave my face a final wipe with the back of my hand, to be sure, and I said, 'That's definitely what we'll do. I'm being very grown-up, Maggie.'

'Yes,' said Maggie. 'You are.'

'I'm going to want lots of praise for this,' I said.

'That can be arranged,' said Maggie.

I didn't ask any more about the baby. I needed time to get used to the idea of what the real problem was. I understood it now. It was that the baby might not end up real, after all, might be going to disappear into misty nothing.

Chapter Ten

It's a bit difficult for me to tell you this, but I felt
really happy on Dartmoor. That sounds as if I'd
stopped caring about the baby – but to be fair to
me you have to remember that the baby was just
a lot of mysterious heavings and nudges to me,
while Mum was Mum.

Everything turned round the other way when I
knew Mum would be OK, as if everything really
was linked.

After what I'd been through in mid-Devon, and
after all the talk of Cranmere Benjie and blanket
bogs, I thought I knew what Dartmoor would be
like – flat and grey and wet and mushy, with a
thick fog over it; a blanket fog on the blanket
bog. I don't think I knew you were allowed to
have a moor without a fog. But you are. Sometimes, anyway. That day it was clear and sunny,
and the moor was a sea of great grassy waves
dotted with little rocky mountains called tors,
and with pretty villages and little fairy-tale
wooded streams here and there. Devon had stopped persecuting me, all right. I felt as though it
was rolling on its back in the sun, like a fat happy
dog.

By lunchtime, when we were sitting at the
edge of Hay Tor, we'd stocked up on socks,

extra-strong mints and sandwiches – all of which was a great comfort to me. We'd telephoned Dad to find there was no change. Maggie had rung Nigel and had a nice time giving him details about the rotten day we'd had thanks to him. Nigel had said that, oddly enough, Michael was cross with him, too, because he'd asked him to find someone to interview who only spoke Cornish and no English. Michael had said there hadn't been anyone like that around for years, and even if there was, how were they supposed to understand each other. Nigel had accused him of negative thinking, and Michael had said that he wanted Nigel to know that in his spare time he was researching the perfect murder. Nigel couldn't understand, he told Maggie, why they were both being so difficult. He also said he was just on his way out to pay Maggie's London money into her account, as promised.

'Will he do it?' I said.

'Who can tell?' said Maggie. 'You might as well try and forecast the weather.'

We had all six maps of Devon spread out around us, twitching in the breeze, and Maggie took pictures with the telephoto lens and pointed things out to me, on the maps or in the world, while she wrote her notes.

She told me about Dewerstone Tor, which they used to think was one of the homes of the Devil. She pointed out Hound Tor, just across from where we were sitting. She said it was supposed to be the Devil's pack of red-eyed hounds, turned into stone in mid-hunt. If I screwed up my eyes, I could just make it look like a line of Mega-Berwicks. I think. She told me about the church just outside Buckfastleigh where Sir Richard Cabell was buried about four hundred years ago, with a huge stone on top of him because he was so all-round evil that the villagers were afraid he might crawl out of his tomb and boggle at them, and how his hunting dogs were so wild and vicious that the stories about them gave Conan Doyle the idea for *The Hound of the Baskervilles*. She told me about Fox Tor Mires, not far from Dartmoor prison, where escaped convicts are supposed to have been sucked down to their deaths, and about a part of the road near a place called Postbridge where people have seen UFO's hovering above their cars, and where one man said that a pair of disembodied hairy hands appeared on the steering wheel and twisted it and made him crash.

I said these stories were terrific to hear in the sun, but I was glad I hadn't known them last night. I did wonder if she was telling them to me now to stop me going off again, but I don't think she'd be so sneaky.

It was quite a strange feeling, getting on with Maggie. She even looked different. I mean, I looked at her little strappy high-heeled red sandals, and I looked at the stony slope we'd walked up from the car down below, and instead of thinking what stupid shoes they were, I thought how amazing Maggie was to be able to walk up there in them. I couldn't do it – I need all the help my trainers can give me.

I said, 'Maggie, after we get back, will you come round more often?'

'Yes, if you like,' she said. 'If you don't mind your Dad and me having political fights.'

'Oh no,' I said, 'I don't mind. I think arguments are quite stimulating really.'

You can see how it was getting. Obviously too good to last. But I didn't realize that until I put my foot in it. Maggie had wheedled a bit of cash out of the bank at Great Torrington, after they talked to her bank back home, but it wasn't a lot and we were back in a credit-card-hotel situation. So that evening we checked in at a small hotel in Torquay, and that's when I did it.

All day we'd been nice to each other, and by the time we got to the reception desk, I was really quite high. I felt I'd got the hang of reality and truth and all those sorts of things, and that I'd worked out how to get the most out of the trip. Who was the stupid child, I was thinking, who'd whined about being rushed around the place, who wasn't able to appreciate the excitement of travelling with a journalist? Most people would envy me, I was thinking. Especially as I wasn't just a hanger-on – Maggie herself had said she thought of me as an apprentice.

Maggie wrote our names in the register and I lounged against the desk and wished I had some gum to chew to complete my image.

Then the receptionist asked The Question. 'On holiday, are you?' she said. Well, Maggie began the bit about 'just touring around' or whatever it was she used to say, but I cut in, didn't I? 'Oh no,' I said, 'my aunt is a very successful journalist. We're down here on a writing assignment.' It came out very well, clearly, loudly, but quite casually.

I don't know what sort of reaction I'd expected, but I had been sure *something* would happen.

The receptionist was one of those 'perfect' ones with shiny hair and shiny eyelids and shiny lips and shiny nails – and probably shiny shoes as well, I suppose I'd hoped she'd look impressed. But all she did was to swing the book around to face her and look to see if Maggie had filled in all the columns properly.

A youngish man coming down the stairs smiled at us – well, I was learning that most men smile at Maggie. The receptionist smiled at us – she had shiny teeth, of course, but I didn't mind that, I've got those, too – and that seemed to be it. What a wash-out, I thought. Then I looked at Maggie and there was something about the way she said we could manage our own bags, thank you, that told me she wasn't very pleased, but I still didn't really know what I'd done.

While we were changing our socks for dinner, or one of us was, I said to Maggie, 'What did I say wrong?'

'Don't worry about it,' said Maggie.

'If I'm an apprentice,' I said, 'I have to be told.'

Maggie was doing quite effective things to her face with a tube of make-up. 'It's just,' she said, with her voice coming out a bit twisted as she made faces at herself in the mirror, 'that life's easier if people don't know what I do.'

'But why? Tell me.'

'There's something about being connected with journalism or publishing that brings out the worst in everybody. You wouldn't believe how many people have got appalling typescripts tucked away that they think I ought to read and advise on or recommend to a publisher. It's no use explaining that I don't have any influence with any publishers, not even the ones I work for, and that I haven't got the time or expertise to sort out their writings for them. They just smile sweetly and tell me I underestimate myself and press crumpled pages into my hands.'

'Maggie, you're on an ego trip,' I said. 'I don't believe people are that interested in what you do.'

Maggie finished her face and blew a kiss at herself in the mirror. 'I wish you were right,' she said. 'Would you like to hear some of the more frequently used openers? There's – "I've had such an interesting life, I feel sure someone like you could make a book out of it" – and there's – "As soon as I have the time, I'm going to write a best-seller, I could really use the money, could you give me any tips, do you think?" – and there's – "I've found this marvellous diary in the attic written by my great-great aunt and illustrated with her own flower sketches, I wonder if you would just glance at it and recommend a publisher." And even, "I'd appreciate some technical advice – do you think it's best to write by hand or directly onto the typewriter?" Do you know, a hotel manager once even asked me to write his brochure for him over dinner.'

'You're exaggerating though, aren't you?'

'No,' said Maggie. 'I'm not even telling you the more extreme ones. I shan't mention the woman who wanted me to read her dog's autobiography because she thought it showed real promise. She'd done the actual writing, you understand, she admitted that, but she said she had only written what she knew he wanted her to say. And I won't tell you about the man who said he

132

knew "The Meaning of Life" and wanted me to get him a wider audience by writing an article on him.'

'What did he say it was, then? The Meaning of Life?'

'He wouldn't tell me unless I guaranteed to publish the article. And I also won't tell you about the woman who wanted my advice on some poems that had been dictated to her by her father from beyond the grave. Oh no, I won't tell you about any of those, you wouldn't believe me.'

'But it doesn't always happen, does it?'

'No,' said Maggie, 'not always. It's just nicer if it doesn't happen at all. And now I'm travelling with you, you see, people don't usually ask. They assume it's a holiday. For once in my life I look normal and I don't have to think up a cover story.'

'It won't happen here,' I said. 'I was expecting some big reaction when I said you were a journalist but no one even twitched.'

'No, that's true,' said Maggie. 'I expect I'm being over-sensitive.'

'Anyway, I'm really sorry,' I said.

I was.

'It's OK,' said Maggie.

It wasn't.

We went down to the bar before dinner – as Maggie got tireder she was eating earlier, I noticed – and the barman got his act going before the tonic hit the gin.

'A journalist, eh?' he said. 'I could tell you some stories. I could write a book about my experiences here.'

'I'm sure,' said Maggie. 'Make that a double, would you?'

She got out her purse.

'On the house,' said the barman.

'I prefer to settle up,' said Maggie.

The barman gave her a huge wink. 'I appreciate that you people aren't supposed to accept freebies,' he said, 'but who's to know?'

Maggie put some cash on the counter. 'That should be about right,' she said. She took her gin and I took my orange and we went and sat at a corner table as far as possible from the bar.

I whispered to Maggie, 'It's probably just that he fancies you.'

She got out her notebook and scribbled in it and then pushed it across the little table at me. 'He just thinks I might write up his bar . . . ' it said in her handwriting.

The youngish man I'd seen on the stairs came in and went up to the bar. The barman ignored him. He was leaning on the bar with both arms and still looking at Maggie. He said, 'You really see life in a place like this.'

'Mm,' said Maggie.

'A straight Scotch, please,' said the youngish man.

The barman took a glass and held it under the upside-down-bottle of whisky behind the bar, but he didn't fill it at once. 'I could give you some anecdotes about customers we've had here,' he said. 'We often get the stars from the summer shows, you know. The up-and-coming ones.'

'No ice,' said the youngish man.

The barman squirted some whisky into the glass and pushed it across the counter to him without even looking at him. I'd have thought the man would have been cross, I would have been, but I could see he was just sort of laughing to himself.

'They're not always very discreet, show business people,' said the barman. 'Not when they've had a few. And I have a very good memory.'

Right at that moment another man came in to the bar. I think he may have been the hotel manager, or perhaps he was the head waiter. He was holding what I thought at first was a photo album. He came straight to our little table and opened the album up and handed it to Maggie and I saw it was the menu. Maggie didn't seem surprized at first, she just took it, but then the man at the bar said, 'Five star service tonight, eh? Don't I get one?'

'Of course,' said the manager, or waiter, or whatever he was, and he looked at the barman, and the barman shrugged and came out from behind his bar and went out of the room.

'May I recommend the fish?' said the manager-waiter to Maggie. He was standing a bit too close to our table, looming over us, rather.

'Look,' said Maggie, 'I'm not writing a food guide, you know.'

'Of course,' said the manager-waiter. 'I quite understand. Now as you will see, fish is the chef's speciality – all caught in the waters around here – and I should like to emphasize that all our vegetables are fresh, except the peas. Over my long years in the business I have discovered that customers genuinely prefer frozen peas. In fact, I understand surveys have been done which indicate that across the country the majority of people prefer frozen peas.'

'And canned sweet corn?' said the youngish

135

man at the bar, as the waiter came back in to the room and handed him his own menu. He took it, but I noticed he didn't read it. I don't think he really wanted it, I think he was just feeling left out.

'It's only fair to tell you,' said Maggie, 'that I'm just writing a straightforward piece on scenery and museums and pubs that do lunches. Hotels don't feature . . .'

'Please!' said the manager-waiter. 'There's no need to explain, I appreciate that it's none of my business. Naturally when the young lady on the desk overheard your . . . your . . . companion's comments, she felt she should pass them on to me, but I shall say no more. I hope that you'll be able to feel you are still travelling incognito.'

What I really hated about that man was that he made it so clear he knew it was all my fault.

'I'll leave the menu with you,' he said, 'we begin to serve dinner in fifteen minutes. Should you wish to ask any further questions, or if perhaps you would care to see the kitchens, you have only to ask.' He smiled and nodded in an annoyingly cunning way, and went out of the bar, and at that exact moment the man with the Scotch began to move, and I could tell he was going to join us. Things were going from bad to worse.

I said quickly, 'Maggie, time to phone for news.' It was, too, that was the beauty of it.

'Oh yes,' said Maggie, 'well remembered.' And she leapt up and vanished. I've never seen anyone move so fast.

The man with the Scotch still came on over to our table, even though Maggie had gone, and asked if he could join me. He had a nice face, but I was getting wise at last. I knew he only wanted to talk to me so as to get at Maggie for something. For all I knew, he had a hand-written spy thriller in his back pocket. So I said I was going to join in the phone call, and I got myself out of there, fast.

Maggie was phoning from our room. We talked to Dad and we talked to Mum, too. Maggie didn't let on what I knew, Dad sounded edgy, I thought, but Mum sounded fine. Nothing was different — then. I didn't feel impatient because I was used to the routine of it by now – move on, phone home, no change, move on . . .

'Do you mind if we eat out?' said Maggie, when we'd hung up. 'I saw a cafe round the corner that's probably cheap enough for me to pay by cash. And I'm not sure I can cope with hearing the personal history of every dish we order.'

The vague food smells coming from the back of the hotel were rather good, but what could I say? If Maggie wasn't going to moan at me for what I'd let out, I could hardly moan about missing the chef's best efforts. So all I said was, 'I hope we can sneak out without being spotted.'

We did, but there was another nasty surprise around the corner. The cafe was small, and greasy, and friendly – but it wasn't licensed.

'Oh Maggie!' I said.

'It's OK,' said Maggie. But I could tell she was flustered because she just ordered the special three-course dinner without even asking what it was. It turned out to be grey chicken soup with bits of pimply skin in it, a sort of bone stew, and a blob of bright pink sweet stuff for pudding which we couldn't identify.

I was glad in one way because I felt less guilty when I'd eaten a really horrible meal, but it was sad to watch Maggie trying to push the rafts of pimples out of the way, and rattling the bones hopefully around in their gravy in search of a piece of meat, and drinking cloudy water.

'Don't look so worried,' she said, putting the bright pink stuff in her mouth rather carefully, as if she wasn't sure what it might do. 'It's all part of life.'

'Not the best part,' I said. 'I'll never drop you in it like that again.'

Maggie just winked at me.

When we got back to the hotel I told her to go straight in and up to our room in case the manager leapt out to invite her to inspect the breakfast bacon. I said I'd get the key and follow her.

The youngish man came out of the dining-room as the second red high-heel disappeared at the top of the stairs. He didn't see her. He came up to me just as the receptionist was reaching round for our key.

'Hello again,' he said. 'I wondered if you and your aunt would like to join me for a drink. There's a nice pub near here where the so-called children's room is actually very pleasant to sit in.'

I liked him for saying that, but I wasn't going to be caught out. I'd switched over to my protective mode, now, and I wasn't going to let anyone get at her for anything.

'Sorry, she's gone up,' I said.

He took a neat little pad and pencil out of his inside jacket pocket and began to write fast. 'All

138

right,' he said, 'but she might change her mind. Could I ask you to give her this, please?'

I had to take the note. I took the key and I backed away from the counter in case the shiny receptionist asked awkward questions about why we'd gone out for dinner.

'May see you later,' said the man.

'No,' I said. What could I do – this one was obviously not going to be easy to put off. Then I had what I thought was a brainwave. 'She definitely won't be down again tonight,' I said, and I came out with a really good excuse for her. I don't know what made me think of it, but I could tell it had worked because he looked a bit startled and then just sort of nodded.

I ran.

Up in our room Maggie showed me the note. It said, 'As one journalist to another, may I recommend announcing yourself as a commercial traveller? Give me a ring in room sixteen if you both feel like coming out for a drink to discuss suitable cover stories. David Johnson. PS at all costs avoid the chef – he has MEMOIRS.'

'What excuse did you give?' said Maggie.

Even before I told her, I knew I'd put my other foot in it.

'I told him you were going to spend the evening waxing your moustache,' I said. 'I don't know why. A girl at school has a mother who does it.'

Maggie sat down on the bed.

'Niece-tricide?' I said.

'You were trying to help,' said Maggie.

'Ring him and tell him I made it up,' I said. 'I'll ring him and tell him I made it up.'

But Maggie put her hand over the phone. 'I

139

just haven't the strength,' she said. 'Dear Clare, I do love you, but I don't know if I prefer you on my side or against me.'

'Can you tell the difference?' I said unhappily.

'Have you got a spare extra-strong mint?' said Maggie. 'My stomach thinks I've declared war on it.'

We both went to bed early, but I lay awake for ages trying to plan our get-away and what we'd do about breakfast.

I needn't have.

The telephone rang in our room at eight that morning, and we left the hotel in such a state that no one would have dared to chat us up about anything at all. As for breakfast, neither of us thought of it until lunchtime.

It was Dad on the phone. He talked to Maggie, then she made him tell me the news himself.

Mum had gone into labour, suddenly, in the night, and they'd done an emergency Caesarian. She was just coming round now. She was fine, he said, absolutely fine. And I had a new baby brother – a perfect and healthy and OK baby brother.

Maggie and I were jumping up and down and laughing so much we could hardly dress and pack.

We managed to calm down a bit before we went down the stairs, but we were still a bit giggly and silly.

As Maggie paid at the desk, I did manage to remember she had a deadline. 'What about Devon,' I said. 'What about the job?'

'I'll come back,' said Maggie. 'I'll stay long enough to greet the new chap and than I'll take you to Linda's – she and her parents are just back, your father says, and then I'll come back down here again.'

'You'll get on better without me,' I said.

'Oddly enough,' said Maggie, 'I shall really miss you.'

Then, just as I was following her out of the front door, I saw David Johnson coming down the stairs.

He looked even nicer now I knew he was one of us. Maggie was coming back to Devon in a day or so, I thought, she might bump into him again. You never can tell. So I ran back across the hall, just for a moment, with the blue bag-tag scratting on my back and the big zip bag banging me on the knee. He stopped at the foot of the stairs and smiled.

'I lied about the moustache,' I said.

Then I turned and scratted and banged out after Maggie.

So that's where we were when we heard you'd arrived safely. That's why we weren't around to welcome you.

I said to Maggie we should drive off into the sunset, that's traditional for happy endings. But she said that as it was eight-thirty in the morning and we were travelling east, this couldn't be arranged.

I'll probably tell you this story again when they say you're old enough to understand it. They say you don't know what I'm talking about now. They say you only look up at me because you hear the sound of my voice and that you only seem to smile at me because you've got wind. That's what they say.

If I do tell you again, when you're older, I hope you won't mind hearing it all twice. Because you know and I know that you understand every word already – just like our old Berwick does.

THE END

ADAM'S COMMON

BY DAVID WISEMAN

Peggy Donovan is horrified when she hears
that the Council are planning to build over
Adam's Common – the beautiful green spur of
unspoilt land stretching right into the heart of
the town. For Adam's Common is the only
thing that she really likes about her new home
and life in ugly, industrial Traverton.

But there is more than just beauty that draws
Peggy to the Common – some mystery, some
long-forgotten secret. Why is it called Adam's
Common? Who once lived in the ruined house
that she feels she must visit again and again?
Who is the strange boy she sees, who seems to
vanish into thin air? Peggy knows only one
thing for sure. She has got to do something to
try and stop the development from going ahead
– even if it means looking for answers from the
past . . .

0 552 52511 1

If you would like to receive a Newsletter about our new Children's books, just fill in the coupon below with your name and address (or copy it onto a separate piece of paper if you don't want to spoil your book) and send it to:

The Children's Books Editor
Transworld Publishers Ltd.
61-63 Uxbridge Road,
Ealing
London W5 5SA

Please send me a Children's Newsletter:

Name..

Address...

....

....

All Children's Books are available at your bookshop or newsagent, or can be ordered from the following address:
Corgi/Bantam Books,
Cash Sales Department,
P.O. Box 11, Falmouth, Cornwall TR10 9EN

Please send a cheque or postal order (no currency) and allow 60p for postage and packing for the first book plus 25p for the second book and 15p for each additional book ordered up to a maximum charge of £1.90 in UK.

B.F.P.O. customers please allow 60p for the first book, 25p for the second book plus 15p per copy for the next 7 books, thereafter 9p per book.

Overseas customers, including Eire, please allow £1.25 for postage and packing for the first book, 75p for the second book, and 28p for each subsequent title ordered.